# THE AGENCY

M.M. GOLDLOVE

Copyright © 2018 M.M. Goldlove
All rights reserved.
ISBN: 9781976797316

# THE AGENCY

M.M. Goldlove

M.M. GOLDLOVE

# 1: The Roof Terrace

People often ask me, 'Chris, how did a nice guy like you get mixed up with The Agency?' If I think they really want to know, this is the story I tell them.

The Agency sprang to life on the Harrods roof terrace, in the heart of Knightsbridge, and looking down over its billionaires' playground of gold-plated penthouses, boutiques-by-appointment, and gentlemen's clubs so exclusive they could have boarded up the doors and pretty much no one would have noticed.

From there, it grew to serve a London I still struggle to understand, and back then would never have recognised in a million years or even imagined possible: a sexual superhighway of a city built on a web of global money, lust and need; a London standing at the churning confluence of the great rivers Wealth and Want, where everything came with a price tag, and nothing was not for sale.

You're probably curious to know how a regular guy from Wembley found himself catapulted into so much tomfoolery. Like most life-changing events, it was all jump-started by coincidence and chance, and a random encounter with one of the most stunning girls I have ever drawn breath next to. She opened my eyes to this secret London, powered by sex, ordered by sex, with its thousand sly conduits, arcane codes and hidden spaces connecting the wealthy people wanting sex to the beautiful people selling it. They say knowledge is power: together we leveraged this secret city for all it was worth, to build one of the most exclusive and sought-after agencies in the city.

But we're getting a bit ahead of ourselves here, so we should go back to where this story really begins, in the days before I cut myself adrift from the real world, swapped decent society for high society, and set sail on London's high sexual seas, with no charts, no compasses, and no real idea of what I was letting myself in for.

To set the scene a little, it was the heat wave summer of 2005, and Londoners were living the best of times and worst of times. On July the sixth that year, tickertape rained down on Trafalgar Square as we celebrated becoming an Olympic city, then just twenty-four hours later the air was filled with dust and ash and we were mourning and trying to make sense of the 7/7 bombings. The two events left their mark, and branded London as a global city. All at once we were opening ourselves to the world, were terrified of the world, seduced and fearful, embracing even as we pulled away.

Back then, I naively thought of myself as a working class boy already made good. I was flogging designer suits five days a week in the menswear department of Harrods, and business was booming. It seemed overnight the city was a giant Neodymium magnet drawing a global elite with time to burn, and money they probably needed to burn, and every day brought new excesses as obscene as they were intoxicating.

Harrods had always oozed refinement: it seeped from its stone cupolas and crenellations, trickled down its faux gothic columns, and pooled discreetly on its chequered marble floors. And refinement drew money, brass chasing class, as they say. From Russia, from the US, and the Middle East, imposing men in tailored suits and flowing robes strode powerfully into the store scanning its far horizons, big game hunters hungry for trophies.

Their consorts, pouty, bored-looking Russian girls and lithe-limbed Latinas, foraged through our glittering display cases, our seductively curated shelves and racks, piling their spoils onto our counters price tags untroubled. Then the big game hunters would be back pulling out their big guns, to the blinding flash of Black Centurion Amex.

This was a golden age in luxury retail, the storm before the calm that descended on the coattails of the financial crash, when cash registers were still ringing like well-mannered Vegas jackpots, with single transactions in the tens of thousands. But it was about so much more than the money. At Harrods we stood tall on the world stage, a revered intersection in time and space where the big players came to indulge and spend recklessly before heading back to their oil-rich deserts and post-perestroika arctic tundra. It was intoxicating.

Not that the job was all sunshine and unicorns, you understand. Luxury retail is seductive and corrosive all at the same time. You'd come to work in your designer suit it would take the best part of a year to save up for, and that in itself would be enough to make you feel great and lousy all at the same time. You'd build a mind-set of super-confidence, pride yourself in providing superior customer service, all the airs and graces, to film stars, sports stars, oligarchs and aristocrats. Your customers might buy into that and make you feel like a million dollars in return, or they could look straight through you like you weren't even there. Or sometimes they'd switch without warning, so you were their confidante one minute and their lackey the next, with no idea of what you'd done or where you stood. And then, when your shift was over, you'd take the bus home to your one bed flat in Wembley, which you knew of course was where you really belonged.

The only part of the day guaranteed to make me feel good about myself was lunchtime, and from late morning there was always the same anxious clock watching, waiting for the vintage department timepiece to stagger around to one. Then the race was on, to the subsidised staff canteen (designer suit, but I couldn't afford Knightsbridge lunches) and a generous dollop of lasagne or carbonara from Nancy the Nigerian cook, so tiny she could barely see over her hotplates. I would always ask how her grandkids were, just to see her smile a smile pretty much as big as she was, then sprint up the grand central staircase, my lunch tray balanced out in front of me, and shoulder the massive glass doors at its apex out onto the joys of the roof terrace.

The Harrods roof terrace was legendary. It spilled out from an arcing dome into an al fresco piazza scattered with benches and tables where everyone – shop girls, security and management - went to eat their lunches, catch up with the mobiles they were forbidden to use in-store on pain of death, read, laugh, gossip or just plain people watch.

When you stepped out onto that rooftop, you were floating on the rising hum of the city. You could stand way at the edge of the terrace and look down on the red buses, the black cabs and chauffeur-driven limos, too many vehicles fighting for not enough road, and watch their angry, ant-like progress through refined Knightsbridge. By early afternoon that overheated summer, the streets way below would already be shimmering, and you could taste the blurry emissions of diesel and the baking pavement as they floated up on the sticky air and were caught and carried on the cooler rooftop currents. It was like being up with the 747s and their vapour trails, and the helicopters whirring above the Thames.

But quite honestly this was only the smallest part of it, just the backdrop, not the show. Guys like me went to the roof terrace for one reason and one reason only: the girls. Every lunch time, the girls from the makeup counters and designer concessions crowded the terrace in a shimmering haze of sexiness, perfectly groomed, coiffed and painted, draped in Givenchy, Armani and Fendi, and trailing a sweet intoxication of Obsession and Eternity. It was like a United Nations of beauty, a frame-by-frame replay of every Miss World pageant I'd ever watched, a lifetime of Bond girls, every race, every nationality, every kind of perfect.

I was transfixed, a willing captive to every sound and gesture, from the clattering rhythm of their stilettoes on the flagstones, to their musical laughter pitching on the breeze. No detail was too small not to be drunk in to the point of intoxication, from the lustre of their sun-lit hair, to the honey sweet curves of their thighs and the graceful taper of their bare legs. These girls cast a spell every day between one and two, which I fell under with wonder, with gratitude, and with a paralysing fear of destroying by doing something as stupid as opening my mouth and actually talking to any of them.

Good luck to the Alpha males up there who were foolhardy enough to play that game! And there were plenty of them: the ex Paras and Royal Marines working in security, huge guys you knew could kill you fifty ways with a pencil; the cocky warehouse guys, East End Del Boys as they were known; and the department managers, red and white carnations pinned to their chests like campaign medals and, like storybook generals, at a slight remove from the hoi polloi. I'd watch the sharks circle, move closer, and attempt some clumsy chat up that generally culminated in rejection and humiliating retreat. Ironically, it was only the gay guys who ever really got to spend time with these goddesses, bitching with them, talking fashion, kissing and hugging and to be perfectly honest really pissing me off.

That summer there was one girl above all the others I was desperate to talk to. Louisa had a real Salma Hayek look: perfect mocha complexion, dark almond-shaped eyes, blood-red lips that parted in a smile that just killed me, and incredible curves that simply didn't quit. No matter where she was on the terrace, she always seemed to be right in my sightline, as if she drew me to her just by being there.

I spent these lunch hours chatting with the security and warehouse guys, or more often than not with my mate Charlie from the toy department, me the cheeky chappy in my designer suit, Charlie distracted and irascible in his bow-tie and red and yellow waistcoat everyone in Toys was forced to wear. Friendships can take root in the most unlikely soil, like those saplings that sprout along derelict rooftops. I'd struck up mine with Charlie initially out of pity: in his uniform, he looked like Ronald McDonald on speed, a misfit even among the misfits of the toy department, where you were encouraged to give off a Mad Hatter energy, but he just looked bug-eyed neurotic. Over the summer we'd gotten into the habit of sharing a lunch time pack of Marlboro Lights on the terrace, two single straight lads talking football and laughing at the madness of guys like us working in Harrods, while we drank in the sexiness of these girls in their cliquey lunchtime groups.

We'd try not to stare too obviously, at the girls in general and Louisa in particular, and our covert operation was exhilarating up to a point, but over time it also became kind of depressing, knowing we'd basically relegated ourselves to rooftop observers in this game of love. These girls were so out of our league, we knew our only chance of dating one was either winning the lottery or getting signed for Chelsea. The odds were much the same either way.

'Mate, her!'

'That one? She's stunning.'

'No, not her, her!'

'Dude, you're staring.'

'You're the one being a bit obvious mate.'

'Whatever, dude. Time for one more cigarette?'

Clock-watching again now, though up here wishing time

would come to a complete standstill, sixty rooftop minutes never enough.

But back to the girls, how did they spend their time? The conversations we strained to hear were a catalogue of boyfriend and work dramas, disputes over rotas, grievances over holiday pay, what someone had promised, what someone else shouldn't have been wearing. Naturally enough though, the conversations we couldn't make out took on a significance way beyond any we could. When a few of the girls' voices grew hushed and colluding, usually when Louisa was at the centre of things, then we'd force our focus twice as hard, hanging on every syllable, desperate to unlock these feminine secrets tumbled in the noises of the city. Slices of intrigue flew through the air bright and blurry as hummingbirds, dropping to our ears as pieces of an elusive puzzle, mysterious key phrases caught, then lost, then caught again.... 'these agencies' ... 'clingy clients' ... 'make a fortune' ... 'fall for you so quickly.'

'Chris...mate!...what are they talking about now?'

'Don't have a clue dude.'

'But are they...'

'Shhhhhut the fuck up Charlie, and maybe I'll be able to tell you.'

'Ok, ok, chill pill dude.'

Our serial cack-handedness, and unerring ability to throw

each other off our game, left this rooftop mystery to marinate; over time it deepened into something as elemental as the air that carried and masked it. Whatever secrets the girls were sharing, why did the fragments never quite make a whole? Take clingy clients, for example. I mean, how clingy could clients get? Demanding sure, complete nightmares on occasion, but emotionally attached, to the point of dependence? Were these girls moonlighting somewhere else, somewhere even more exclusive than Harrods? And if the pay there was as good as they hinted, firstly why were they still here, and secondly shouldn't I be getting in on the action? Always there though, hidden in the whispers and half-glances, the hint of a different explanation.

Well, our lunchtimes drifted in this bittersweet dream of beautiful girls and elusive secrets, and then one day it just happened. Louisa, stunning Louisa, a vision in her Louboutin heels, a perfect hourglass in her fitted Chanel suit, sexy, mysterious Louisa, who held the Harrods roof garden and all its secrets in the palm of her hand, spoke. To me.

This event is branded to my memory like the inked name of a never-forgotten first love, so that even now, more than a decade later, I can talk you through it frame by epic frame. Louisa was perched on a bench just across from where I was smoking on the terrace, fumbling through a Chanel bag for something it was becoming progressively clear wasn't there.

Abandoning the search, she looked across the walkway of adjacent benches that separated us, me alone on my side and she alone on hers, smiled enquiringly in my direction and asked in her seductive Latina accent, 'Do you have a light?

And in that moment, as time temporarily vanished, as the city held its noisy breath and the terrace shrank away to nothing, all I could think was that I wasn't worthy. But it was now or never. I steeled myself, rose unsteadily to my feet and made a kind of inadvertent courtly bow in her direction as I reached out to her with my Clipper lighter's budding flame. I can still see her perfect lips purse to inhale the flickering heat, then gift me the most stunning smile in return. I smiled back, and started wracking my brains for the words that would hold her where she sat for just a little longer.

Ten minutes later, and I'd made more progress with her in that short period than I had with any girl I'd spoken to that summer. My tactics, for once, had been perfectly on point. Step one, I'd used the excuse of the busy walkway to move across and join her on her bench, then step two I'd lit her another couple of cigarettes in quick succession as I had asked her where she was from, what it was that had brought her to London, and about her career with Chanel.

From there I'd run out of steps, but we'd jumped scattershot from talking about Harrods and its old-fashioned hierarchies to laughing at the madness of carnival in Rio. By this point I was working without a net, totally hers, already in love with her laughter, her wicked personality, and the mischievous sparkle behind those beautiful eyes.

And either I was seriously oxygen-deprived and delirious in the thin rooftop air, or this stunning woman was having fun with me too. Not that I thought she was flirting with me. I mean, I was a fairly decent-looking chap back then in my sharp suit, and with my winning smile, but Harrods had a way of letting you know where you stood in the order of things, crammed with its six foot plus model boys working the tills between castings. We were cracking jokes though, totally relaxed with each other, and she was clearly enjoying my cheekiness and sense of humour, the stuff I liked about myself, and that marked me out from the other guys on the roof terrace with their clumsy, obvious advances.

And after that, of course, I couldn't stop thinking about Louisa, and wanting to talk to her again. Not that it was easy. The next time I saw her, she was surrounded by a large group of girls, all with cigarettes in their hands, all gossiping, and all annoyingly with lighters of their own, and I was back to snatching up crumbs of conversations as I sat close by, half-heartedly chatting with some of the warehouse guys.

As the weeks wore on though, I took every opportunity I got to talk to her, and whenever we did talk, the conversation always just seemed to flow. It turned out that we were both storytellers, and we loved swapping tales about Rio and London. She would tell me about her love affair with her new home city, her apartment in South Kensington (fuck, she'd only been here two years and already lived in South Ken; I'd been here all my life and still bussed home every night to Wembley) and I'd tell her about growing up here with my mixed bag of friends. The one thing we didn't talk about – she didn't volunteer and I still didn't have the balls to ask her - was those secret conversations. I also didn't mention my own little secret: that I was steadily falling for her. I'm sure she could tell I was checking her out, even though I tried not to, but it was impossible not to look, and we both somehow pretended not to notice.

But all this hushed conspiring between her and the other girls was killing me. Louisa and I were friends now, and we were really starting to open up to each other about our lives. If she had secrets she was confiding to other people on the roof terrace, then why not me? So, one lunch time, towards the end of one of our sprawling conversations, and when we were pretty much by ourselves, I finally summoned the courage to ask her.

She narrowed those beautiful eyes, and held my gaze for a couple of seconds, maybe longer, without saying a word. Then, looking very deliberately over my shoulders, first left then right, so I felt like Roger Moore in Live and Let Die, about to be gifted the secrets of his very own Solitaire, 'Please keep this to yourself,' she whispered, 'I'm an escort.'

Her eyes stared into mine for the longest time, weighing me up I think, deciding if I was a worthy confidante, second guessing how I was going to respond. And, after a long, anxious pause, spent trying to make sense of what I had just been told, what I actually came out with was 'What's an escort?'

'Seriously?' She sounded incredulous. 'Are you kidding Chris? You don't know what an escort is?'

I could feel my cheeks flushing as I gave a single, shamefaced shake of the head.

'Oh my God, you *really* don't know?' Fortunately she was laughing by this point, taking pity on me and choosing to see the funny side. 'You *do* know what a call girl is, right?'

And suddenly the penny dropped. 'Oh my God, I'm so sorry, I don't know what to say,' was the best I could manage this time around. I was totally at sea, only knowing for sure the worst thing I could be doing was apologising.

'Sorry, I really shouldn't have asked,' I apologised once again. Fuck!

'Don't be silly honey,' Louisa smiled, shrugging away my flustered embarrassment. 'Hey, I'm a high-class escort. It's no big deal, it's fine.'

Ok, so now I knew an escort was a call girl. But then,

what did I really know? That world was a complete mystery to me. Thinking hard, all I could relate it to right then was a trip to Amsterdam with some mates, a couple of lads sneaking away to the red light district at three in the morning, and coming back with sordid stories I could barely take in, I was so stoned. I'd only ever had girlfriends, girls who went for normal, run of the mill guys like me. And I just kept thinking someone like Louisa couldn't possibly be a call girl in the sense I understood it. Was there still a chance something had been lost in translation?

'Right. So what's this all about?' I backpedalled, still looking for her to supply a different explanation. 'Someone pays you to go to dinner with them, or to join them at the theatre?'

'Um, sometimes, but there's a bit more to it....' Louisa smiled patiently.

Was Louisa really telling me what I thought she was telling me? And if she was, *why* was she was telling *me*? Choosing *me* to confide in? And what was I supposed to say in return to make this ok, show I was fine with it, even if I really wasn't sure that I was?

I watched Louisa reach into her Chanel handbag and pull out a velvety-black business card, the name AMANDA embossed across its surface in powerful silver letters, and a phone number and website address printed beneath. 'This is the name I go by when I'm working,' she said, pressing it into my hand. 'Maybe you want to take a look.'

THE AGENCY

# 2: South Ken Samba

On the way home to Wembley that night, Louisa's bombshell was still sending out its aftershocks, in a disorienting pact with the scattered sunlight flickering across the bus windows. Sunk deep in her secret, I'd be thrown into the evening rush-hour for a second, as we hit a speed bump, or a tree branch scraped the side of the bus, then plunged back into its giddy free fall.

 Knightsbridge became Wembley far too quickly, and it was only blind instinct that saw me leaping from the bus at the right bus stop. Almost running the couple of streets to my flat, I fumbled with my key in the lock, looking down at hands literally shaking, then stepped over Bubbles and straight to my Dell, only guiltily backtracking to fork some cat food into her dish once the computer was noisily booting up. Then, heart thumping, I keyed in the web address from the business card that had been pressed against my chest all afternoon.

 And there she was. Louisa. Or was it Amanda? That same lovely, familiar face, and those same mischievous eyes staring out from the glare of the screen. Louisa's trademark Chanel suits had been stripped away though, to uncover stockings and suspenders, and silky lingerie that draped Amanda's spectacular body and incredible boobs. I found myself just staring at the screen, hating myself for staring all the while I stared, but simply not able to stop myself. Fuck! Those photos! That body!

Some of the photos focused exclusively on those incredible curves; others drew back a little to show off expensive-looking props and a high-end studio. It was one more space that Louisa made completely her own. It made no difference if she was standing face-on to the camera, or reclining on a theatrical-looking chaise longue. I clicked back through all of these photos, taking in their erotic charge and the sheer professional quality of them. Then, scrolling past her bio and location, I found her fees. She charged an astronomical five hundred pounds for a one-hour in-call. That was more than I earned at Harrods in a week! It certainly explained the mystery of the South Ken apartment.

I could feel my chest tightening just as it had that afternoon on the roof terrace. Forcing my eyes shut, and taking long, deep breaths in an attempt to slow everything down a bit, I tried to make sense of what I'd just seen. Or was it everything I'd just been shown?

Who *was* the girl posing in this studio? Advertising on this website? Was she really the same goddess I'd worshipped from afar on the Harrods roof terrace? The same girl I'd spent the last few weeks thinking I was actually getting to know? And this world set out in front of me right now? Of supermodel escorts, and guys paying thousands for an evening in their company? How, in all my twenty-eight years, could I have remained so totally blind to it!

I mean, I wasn't stupid, I knew about call girls, hookers, whatever you wanted to call them. When I thought about it, there were even a couple of dodgy saunas in Wembley that I'd walk past on the way to friends' houses. They gave off a bit of a sleazy air, and occasionally you'd see a guy ducking in or out, looking a bit shifty and adding to the despondency of it all. But this London of model-beautiful escorts, who worked from luxury apartments? Apartments where a guy like me could lose his head, and his life savings, in a single evening? This secret world was something else, something I'd never even considered might be out there. And yet here it all was, obligingly set out in front of me in glorious technicolour.

\*

It was a couple of days before we ran into each other on the roof terrace again and, when we did, there was a beat of adjustment as the Amanda from the website shape-shifted back to the Louisa I knew. Unless I was imagining it, Louisa hesitated for a second too, before she was back smiling that crazy killer smile. 'Hey Chris, did you have a look at my site? Are you going to come and see me one day?' she teased, a seductive little pout morphing into an irresistible giggle.

'Oh my god, yes, I did, you looked amazing Louisa,' I admitted, smiling in her direction without quite being able to hold her eye. 'I'm afraid I don't have that kind of money though.' Then, almost as an afterthought, 'God, do guys seriously spend that?'

'London's full of wealthy clients,' she answered in a voice not much above a whisper, twisting around as she spoke to check who else might be listening in. Turning back to me, we shared a smile of what I think was nervy complicity. It was like right at this moment we understood she was being Louisa, but we both knew now she was hiding someone else too. It was my turn to scan the terrace. Like how many other of these girls, I wondered, my mind expanding to take in the possibilities of this parallel universe, this secret other city being opened up to me.

I was sitting next to a call girl, a stunning high class escort, who in a couple of hours would leave her Harrods makeup counter, head to her luxury South Kensington apartment and...what? How did these two worlds fit together? What were their rules of conduct and passage? Now Louisa had included me in her secret, was I permitted to ask these sorts of questions? In fact, after she'd trusted me with it, would it be more insulting not to?

'So what sort of guys?' I asked, testing the waters.

'All types of guys, but wealthy guys obviously,' she joked, relaxing now, but her voice kept low. 'I'm very busy, and that's because I'm very good at what I do.' Another complicit little smile.

'Isn't it risky though?'

'Ha, that's so sweet of you Chris,' the touch of her hand now over mine, 'but no, not really, not at the level I work. And you know what? I actually love what I do. And the money's unbelievable too. I mean, I get to travel a lot, and that's great, I've had business trips to Cannes, Vegas and Dubai, but honestly it's all about the money, and it's all about London. This is where the real money is.'

*

In the few minutes I'd spent outside Louisa's apartment block, getting up the nerve to speak into the intercom, three cabs had already drawn up to this same stretch of South Kensington curbside. Each in turn had dispatched its elegantly dressed fares to the same Japanese restaurant on the corner. I had watched them all step out into the floaty summer evening and disappear into its elegant interior, envying all that careless entitlement.

The invitation, like the business card, had come out of the blue, a jolt to the easy rhythm of lunchtime confidences Louisa and I had by now established. Here I was, painstakingly casual in probably the sixth outfit I'd tried on that evening, and almost sick with nerves and excitement. I was finally about to see Amanda's world.

Her apartment door, when I finally got to it, was part open to the corridor in a sort of qualified welcome. Through the gap, I could see a stunning blonde girl, in tiny denim shorts and cut-down t-shirt, dancing barefoot with a well put-together, olive-skinned guy. They were pressed together in a tangle of swinging hips and fast feet, their moves matched to a Latin beat pulsing from a plasma TV that threw out a soft light around them, and a group of less committed dancers. The girl, noticing me, smiled an uninhibited smile, mouthed something I couldn't hear over the Samba, then broke away from the guy and skipped over in a parody of loose-limbed welcome.

'Hey,' you must be Chris,' she said, surprising me with a full-on hug. 'I'm Giselle, Louisa's flatmate. She has told me a lot about you, friend from work right?' And taking my hand, she led me into the party's swell of noise.

The apartment itself was large, high-ceilinged and open plan, all cream walls, white wool carpets and white furniture. Everything about it discreetly shouted class, from the subtle spotlighting and art deco corner lamps to the large mirrors with their elegant bevelled edges and gilt frames, and the cherry wood marquetry of a floor-to-ceiling fireplace. There was a large glass table at one end of the room loaded with food, wine, champagne, spirits and beautiful tableware, and at the other end the floating island of an ultra-modern kitchen, all brushed steel surfaces, was loaded with more. Between these extremities, panoramic French windows opened up the far wall and let out onto a balcony, a cool summer breeze catching at their floor length curtains so they billowed inwards, carrying the falling light of the August evening.

The party was already in full swing: a stunning group of girls were sambaing in the middle of the room where Giselle had been dancing, another group hovering around the glass table, and a third, as with every great party, were over by the kitchen, with its distinctive meaty smells of Brazilian cooking. My eyes instinctively drew to Louisa, dancing with an arm around another girl's waist, in a strappy summer dress that fell lazily over her stunning curves. Catching her eye, I smiled a crooked smile which I hoped conveyed at least a modicum of cheeky charm, and she smiled back and teasingly danced over.

'Chris,' she threw her arms into the air and then around me, squeezing me to her. 'I didn't think you were going to come.'

'What, and miss out on all of this?' Her soft cheeks brushed mine in two almost kisses.

She offered to get me a drink, and when I asked her what she had, she smilingly shouted back 'everything!' The word seemed to hang there as, with a slight turning of her head, she took in the table loaded with its drinks and dishes, the apartment with its beautiful guests, and the panoramic view of the Central London skyline.

'Well, a vodka and Red Bull would be great,' I laughed, as I took it all in too.

While she was mixing my drink, she was busily introducing me to a couple of her other friends as 'Chris my lovely friend from work,' and then, no sooner had she handed it to me than she was gone, promising to be right back.

With Louisa vanished, I was launched into the party proper, carried from guest to guest on its slick Latin currents; firm handshakes, noisy introductions and passionate hugs and kisses crashing against a wall of raised voices and even louder music. It was an insane induction, as waves of hot girls and guys appeared from nowhere to introduce themselves and make me feel welcome, and I smiled and applied my beginners' Portuguese to the task in hand.

At some point the solid Brazilian guy I'd seen dancing with Giselle had his arm tightly wrapped around my shoulder, and was asking me questions he would go on to answer for himself before I could get anywhere near them. 'So you work in Harrods with Louisa? Dude, that's too cool,' he'd ask and answer. 'You get to meet film stars? Footballers? Man, that's awesome!' I was feeling both a little redundant and a bit of a star myself.

And then, after maybe twenty minutes, the noisy current spilled into a deep, calm pool and there at the end of it was Louisa, in front of me again and drawing me to her, and looking so lovely I struggled not to look away. I'm not sure why, but now I was seeing myself through her eyes. Here in this room, surrounded by all these beautiful, charming people, I was the pale, unexceptional Englishman from work, who really shouldn't have accepted her pity invitation, and certainly shouldn't still be here.

'Great party Louisa,' I shouted over the music, 'and I love your flat, and you have some great friends. Think I'm going to have to leave soon though.'

'Are you kidding Chris?' she frowned in mock disapproval. 'The party's just beginning.' And, refusing to take no for an answer, she grabbed my hand and led me through the sea of beautiful faces to the floating island at the kitchen end of the room. A guy there was nonchalantly cutting professional-looking lines of coke, very fat and straight, on some sort of rectangular marble block.

'Would you like some?' she asked, as if she was offering me a cup of tea.

'Ah thanks Louisa, but coke's not really my thing,' I laughed, my hand still in hers. 'It's too moreish, it'll write off my weekend.'

'Ok let's go out onto the balcony and have a cigarette,' she bossed, leading me out into the cooler evening air. 'Another drink?' I shook my head. 'Ecstasy? You've taken ecstasy before, right?'

'Louisa, I grew up during the nineties, the whole rave scene, I've done my fair share,' I couldn't help bragging a little. 'Yeah, I guess I can do an E.'

I watched her take that in, then head over to a narrow console on the other side of the French windows, slide open a small drawer, and return with a plastic sachet from which she squeezed out a small tablet.

'Ah, maybe a half for me,' I said, feeling a bit of a lightweight after my boast. She placed the pill between her lips and bit down on its bisecting groove. 'Don't worry, we're gonna have a ball,' she said, passing me the remaining half with what felt like a smile of real affection. My last really coherent thought was that if I took Ecstasy I had an excuse to stop drinking. That way at least I'd be sure not to do anything stupid.

    I should admit here that, from this point onwards, my memories of the party are vivid, but messy and non-linear, like those dreams you wake up from and spend ages failing to piece together. I know I came up on the E in about fifteen minutes flat. Louisa was still with me at that point, so close in fact I could feel the heat coming from her. And then suddenly she wasn't there, and then she was there again, her Latina accent washing through me but the words somehow missing. Then she was gone for what felt the longest time, and I was buzzing with the music, and an apartment that started to take on a life of its own.

I remember leaning on the floating island of the kitchen, my jaw slackening, and my voice softening and distancing so I wasn't sure if I was speaking my thoughts to myself, or just thinking them. I could hear the guy with the knife cutting more lines of coke. The sound was like a stylus scratching vinyl. Then a two-four Samba beat was rising in waves, soaring into the air and then shattering into shards of pure sound. I was staring at the kitchen ceiling where these fireworks were detonating, then transfixed the beams of light carving hyper-geometric patterns out of the plates and glasses scattered all around me.

And then Amanda, or was it Louisa, was standing next to me again, so close I could feel my arm suddenly against her waist. And I was thanking God, either out loud or in my head, that I'd had the guts to talk to her, because it had led me here to this party, to her and her friends and one of the most amazing nights of my life. Her voice was entering me again, but now making inroads into the insular spell the E had been weaving.

'Come and join me on the balcony,' Louisa was saying,

leading me by the hand to the shock of being back outside and in the cooler air. The giddy, molecular excitement was slowly giving way to a more expansive calm and I could feel the city and the night sky almost silently building around us, a complete universe unfolding and expanding. I remember the balcony had the most incredible view over Central London, and I could even see the Harrods building, spot-lit like an anchoring north star in this vast, velvety galaxy. Louisa put her hand on my chest, I think just to remind me she was there, and asked me how I was feeling. 'Great, thank you!' I answered, elated, before she'd even finished asking the question, so our voices overlapped, like a retreating wash into a breaking wave, and we both laughed. 'Chris, you don't need to thank me, I love having you here,' she murmured, her face next to mine, her lips inhaling from a joint that was suddenly there in the way that things are when you dream them. I remember thinking we must be floating on an ocean of serotonin.

'You have an amazing life Louisa, and this apartment is lovely,' I said, in a voice I still wasn't totally convinced she could hear, it was like I was listening to my own ghost. She shrugged away the compliment. 'This is what escorting has brought me,' she said, 'I've worked very hard for this.'

I took a drag on the joint, now pressed between *my* lips. 'I can't believe we're here, now, talking like this, you know?' I said, the thought trailing away, then another taking its place.

## THE AGENCY

'But clearly you must make great money. And this is all from your site?'

'Not all, I work with agencies too.'

'So how the hell does that work?' I asked. 'What are they? Pimps?'

'Not pimps,' she laughed dismissively, 'but agents who I work with. The majority are British women, some former escorts themselves. And there are a handful of guys in the business too. Do you know what hun,' she placed her cool hand on top of mine, 'I think you would run a great agency.'

'What?! Louisa, I wouldn't even know where to start,' I snorted, laughing into the cool air.

'Well, you are talking to an expert here,' she smiled, 'I do know one or two things. And I have a lot of friends. I know at least six girls in South Ken alone who would work with you, and others all over Central London. You know my flatmate Giselle's also an escort right? The girl who greeted you at the door?'

'Right. Hold it there, I need the loo. Be right back,' I said, my mind working a lot faster than the rest of me as I stumbled to my feet. And then I was floating past her smiling friends towards the bathroom, knowing it was only momentum that was keeping me upright, the way swimming keeps you from sinking. I pushed the bathroom door closed and slumped down onto the toilet seat, ears ringing in the sudden silence.

Me, running an agency? Had Louisa been serious? I was staring at my reflection in the wall-sized mirror across from me, expensive-looking bottles cluttered at its base like their own mini London skyline. Pale face, clammy skin, more than a little unfocused about the eyes. Hardly the look of a successful entrepreneur. But then this party, the laughter, the beautiful guests, who wouldn't want to live like this?

As I was working my way unsteadily back towards the balcony, I caught a single glimpse of the most incredible bedroom: subtle mood lighting, art on huge canvases, a mirrored wardrobe that receded along the entire length of one wall, in an almost infinite line of perspective, and spot-lit at its centre an unbelievable king size bed. If only that room could talk, I thought, laughing to myself, what a story it could tell. Fuck, this was so the life I wanted! And this was the thought I was holding on to, still laughing to myself, as I stumbled back to Louisa standing alone on the balcony.

And this was how we had our first talk about agencies, sitting on a South Kensington balcony in the early hours of the morning, ever so slowly coming down from Ecstasy, as we passed a joint between us and a slow pulsing dawn cut into the night, coming up in tiny throbs.

For once we were totally alone, away from the prying eyes of the Harrods rooftop, and Louisa was saying everything I guess I'd been wanting to hear from her all summer: how sweet I was, how much her friends loved me, and how much she loved having me here. And then she was extending the thought, telling me how wasted I was in Harrods, how I deserved so much more, should take the plunge and set up an agency of my own, earn some real money.

And I was so happy right at that moment, floating in all that love and affection, I just didn't want our conversation to end. 'But what about the law?' I heard myself ask, my voice still coming out oddly distant.

'Chris, do you really think the police give a fuck? They don't care about the high-end stuff. They know there's no coercion. It's just business. And pretty good business at that.'

'But I'm really not sure I'm comfortable with this thing of basically being a pimp.'

'Baby, how many times!' she laughed away her exasperation. 'I already explained, you wouldn't be a pimp. You'd be a middleman, setting up people for companionship. Seriously, it's pretty straightforward, another form of high-end sales, with the sorts of clients you're already used to dealing with in Harrods. You're cute, you're very sweet, I know the girls would love you. I think you'd be perfect.'

'Ha, well, that's a lovely reference Louisa,' I interrupted her, ' but I just don't think I've got what it takes. And then, what about the money? What would it cost to set something like this up?'

'How much you got?' she asked with typical directness.

I did a messy mental calculation of everything I had: my current account, my savings account, the cash I had stuffed at the back of my sock drawer for emergencies.

'Um? About three four grand, give or take?' I exaggerated a bit, but still with a note of apology in my voice. Pretty much what I guessed Amanda could earn in a couple of days.

'I think that's enough to get you started,' she said. 'You'll need a website, and to set up advertising. Open an agency hun, I really think you could make it work.'

Her voice running on, running through me, the two of us laughed together at this crazy idea. But weirdly, as I watched her arguing, elaborating, making it sound so natural and normal, it all started – like this party, this view, this whole night - to make complete sense.

# 3: Sun, sea and web design

The streets were deserted and almost silent, just a couple of sparrows somewhere chirping an argument or love song, and the clatter of my own shoes down the shiny steps from Louisa's. This early, South Ken was a different place, a silent, unguarded citadel. A low summer mist was clinging to the corners of tall buildings, like bits of sleep they were still shaking off, and the first sounds of the wealthy breaking their slumber, a sturdy door, a purring engine, were only beginning to cut through the early light.

As I set out towards Knightsbridge, I was yawning the first jawbreaker yawn of my comedown. It was cut short by the surreal vision of a road full of sleeping supercars, Lamborghinis, Porsches and Ferraris, their sleek curves bumper to bumper in a king's ransom of an arc that stretched from the apartment block all the way to the horizon. Louisa's world!

By the time I'd made it back up to the Brompton Road, Harrods, shut up on itself and its treasures safely locked away, was being lit by the first yellow rays of the morning. Walking past on a Saturday and not going in felt as good as bunking off school. I caught a near empty bus from just outside, which never happened, no screaming school kids, none of the usual fighting for a seat, just a few mute clubbers and shift-workers.

Sprawled out over my seat, with its musty depot smell, I was still carrying the euphoria from the party; that kind of happiness that shines up all the possibilities in you, leaves you feeling invincible for a bit. But as the bus headed back to Wembley, and North West London heaved into focus with its crappier shops and houses, messed up streets and derelict gardens, Louisa, and the party, and our conversation on the balcony were all starting to feel a bit less real.

And by the time I'd let myself into my flat, and was staring blankly at its four walls, the party seemed a world away. For the last five years, this place had been my bachelor pad. I'd ironically christened it my 'man cave'. And after just one night at Louisa's that was exactly how it looked, with its rough walls and sagging sofa, cluttered desk and clapped-out TV.

There were the muffled sounds Wembley made early on a Saturday morning, the stop-start of sirens, and overhead the soft thumps of my neighbours getting their weekend underway. Pulling open my curtains, I took in the familiar 'view', a neighbouring block of flats so close it overflowed the window, just a hint of Wembley stadium peering over its flat roof. I caught myself thinking about the view from Louisa's balcony, that pulsing London skyline that just a few hours earlier I'd watched unfolding with all its silent possibilities.

By now, comedown tiredness was riding me with a vengeance, all mixed up with this newfound despondency at my old life. I drifted over to my bed, and just let myself fall into my duvet. It was like sinking into a consoling cloud.

*

I'd thought I'd be out for the count the whole of Saturday, but by mid-afternoon I actually couldn't have been wider awake. Lying across my bed in a rippled pool of the discarded t-shirts from the night before, my mind was racing through everything that had happened at the party, from the moment I'd arrived at Louisa's right up to arriving back home again, the recaptured excitement of it all burning off my comedown. The ecstasy buzz, the music, the mind-bending conversation on the balcony, they had all come together to produce something really special, one of the best and biggest nights of my life, in fact.

It was the conversation with Louisa on the balcony that kept on looping through my head though. Entering her world had made me see what she did in a totally different light. Not only that, but she had made setting up an agency of my own sound so plausible. Not easy maybe, but challenging and exciting, not to mention the chance to make a shed load of money.

So what was holding me back? Was it I didn't trust her judgement, or that I didn't trust my own when I was around her? If she'd told me I'd make a great acrobat, I should join the circus, would I have believed her any less, and been on the verge of throwing in my career to take trapeze lessons? If I was going to do this thing, it would have to be because *I* wanted it, not because Louisa wanted me to want it. And I was actually starting to think I could run my own agency. She may have said it, but I was starting to believe it.

I was a single guy heading into my late twenties, an age where you start thinking about who you really are and what you want out of life. I'd dropped out of school and into retail at seventeen, without giving it a second thought. The truth was it had never been a passion, or even an ambition. It had always just been work. From my first job stacking shelves on Kilburn High Road, I'd slogged my way up the retail pyramid because, well, that was what you did. And now here I was at the pinnacle, at Harrods, selling luxury menswear in a designer suit I had to save up for months to afford, even with my Harrods discount. Was that it for me?

I'd always secretly imagined myself running something someday, a voice in my head telling me it was all about being your own boss, have a dream of your own or you end up living someone else's. But then life knocks you around a bit, and in retail you get so used to being told what to do, you fall out of the habit of thinking for yourself. And life, as someone once said, happens while you're busy making other plans. So here I was, a bit of a Jack the Lad, everyone's friend, running fast, but where was it actually getting me?

Maybe it was time to take a few risks. Louisa had shown me the rewards that were out there: South Ken apartments, amazing parties, really cool people and nights like last night. All out there for the taking, if I truly wanted them. Since that afternoon she'd dropped her bombshell, she had turned my life upside-down, and that way round it was starting to make a lot more sense. Time to make a leap with my Solitaire, let the cards fall where they may.

So, on that comedown Saturday I took if not exactly a leap, then one small step at least towards my new life. Firing up my trusty Dell, I typed 'London escort agencies' into Google. Google came back with twenty four thousand, two hundred and eleven items (the number today, if you're interested, is closer to a million). They shone a light on a network of businesses that extended from the West End all the way to the outer suburbs and beyond, and an industry accommodating every sexual need, desire and whim. You name it, you could find it: Busty Escorts, Ebony Escorts,

Mature, Dominatrix. It was three the next morning before I called it a night, and after a few hours' sleep, I was back at my computer on the Sunday, researching harder than I ever had at school, absorbing services, prices and locations like a sponge.

And that was how things went on. For the next couple of days, I sleepwalked through work, the usual gossip about a celebrity at the other end of the store, or the new ranges winging their way from Milan, barely registering. I only really came to when I got home. I'd feed the cat, forget to feed myself, and the rest of the evening and well into the night I'd be on my PC, now systematically researching London's agencies, elite to low end, girls charging from the hundreds to the thousands, the city bursting at the seams, every shape and size, nationality, taste and fetish. God knows what Google made of my search history!

It wasn't just a case of learning what was out there, but of working out how I could use that knowledge to distinguish my agency from those twenty odd thousand other links. With all this information overload, how did you make a new agency work? Make people see you, and want you? I already had a pretty good idea of what I wanted, and an even clearer idea of what I didn't. If I was going to do this, I wanted my agency to be built around escorts like Louisa and Giselle, stunning women who knew what they wanted too and how to get it, had a handle on the job and made it work for them. My agency's

## THE AGENCY

Unique Selling Point would be its commitment to the very highest standards of British customer service. If there was one thing both Louisa and I understood, after all, it was that. Together, we would provide the sort of elite service that would distinguish us for all the right reasons.

But to impress clients, you had to have clients to impress in the first place. When I clicked onto other elite websites, I'd try to get a feel for the professionals behind their elegant façades; the designers behind the web pages and the photographers behind the portfolios. These were the people I would need to get on side if I was going to make this happen. Louisa had told me there were a handful of really talented designers responsible for the websites of the top agencies and the best girls, and when I saw anything genuinely stylish, the sort of site I'd want for an agency of my own, it was the same few names cropping up over and over.

On my next day off I started contacting these big guns. It was a sobering experience, like going up against seasoned street fighters. They jabbed me with jargon, blindsided me with talk of logos and fonts, threw in keyword and SEO uppercuts, and when I was punch-drunk and reeling, they lined me up for the knock-out blow, delivering a quote of on average a couple of grand. I'd known it wasn't going to be cheap, I mean web design was still a cutting-edge skill back then, not something teenagers knocked up in their bedrooms, and I'd guessed there'd be a premium for industry discretion. But they were talking pretty much my entire savings just to build site. I was still running fast, getting nowhere.

And then I found Barry. By now I was pitching myself from the outset as someone serious about setting up an elite agency, but needing someone affordable. No point wasting both our times if, like the others, he was going to quote a fortune. When I'd ended this little speech, a beat of silence on the other end of the line was broken by a gravelly chuckle.

'Fair play t'yer, mate! And you're an English guy, that's a bit of a rarity these days. It's been a year at least since I've known a Brit wanting to set up an agency,' he said, his strong estuary vowels clearly marking him as a member of the same club. After some toing and froing, and discussion of costs, 'Look, let's not mess about,' he said, 'why don't you come out to me and let me show you what I can do for yer. Do you know Southend?'

'I do Barry, I used to spend some of my Bank Holidays down there with my mates,' I shot back gratefully.

'Really? Nice one.' I was getting a good feeling about Barry.

My next day back at Harrods was the first lunchtime I'd had a chance to see Louisa since the night of the party. I couldn't wait to see her again, and take her to one side to tell her how much she'd sold me on the agency idea, and how much I'd already achieved. When I mentioned Barry, and the plan to meet him that weekend, I loved that she was even more excited than I was. He had said over the phone the site could be up and running within a month, and she clearly loved that. 'You're going to catch the busiest time of the year, the run-up to Christmas,' she whispered, giving me the most festive of hugs.

*

Sunday rolled around with a holiday excitement. By late morning, I was on a crowded train pulling out of Fenchurch Street, and Southend-bound along with what felt like half of London, the grey verticals of the city giving way to rolling green hills and finally dipping to the end point of the Essex coast.

As we'd arranged, Barry was waiting for me outside Southend station, leant back against his Range Rover, its supersized chrome wheels throwing back the midday sun. Mid-forties, shaven-headed and his eyes blanked out behind gold-rimmed Ray-Bans, he swung an outsize arm in my direction, gently crushing my hand in his own. I had to admit he really looked the business, head to toe in Ralph Lauren, and his polo shirt tight across his chest and biceps. A swirl of tattoos cascaded down his right arm all the way to his wrist, where it met up with a chunky Rolex. And not just any Rolex, but a black-faced gold Submariner. It was love at first sight, for the Rolex and the Range Rover.

We drove down to and jostled along the baking seafront, the townward side crammed with arcades and greasy spoons, and Union Jack-plastered pubs, the air thick with cooking fat and sugar, and the swooping and squawking of gulls. Out to sea, the beach was heaving, and the water dazzling little crests of light all the way to the horizon.

At the end of the seafront, the Range Rover veered up a steep, cambered road that was soon all wilderness, sun-scorched savannah grasses leaning in from either side. After half a mile or so, the car pulled up abruptly outside cast-iron gates that broke a line of high red brick wall. Barry scuffled about for his remote. 'We're here mate,' he stated the obvious, as the gates parted with a soft whir, and the Range Rover lurched to a sudden halt on the gravelled drive of a ranch-style, pitch-roofed bungalow perched on a hilltop overlooking the coast. The bling, the tats, the Range Rover, the secluded location, it wasn't a moment of panic exactly, but it was all starting to feel a bit surreal.

I followed Barry into the bungalow, everything still and silent, like walking into a frozen crime scene, and down some steps into his half basement office-studio. Every wall and surface down there was crammed with memorabilia. Framed England and West Ham shirts. Henry Cooper's signed boxing gloves. Classic movie posters, a couple of great Bond ones. On the far side of the room there was an aquarium that covered the best part of a wall, tropical fish emerging from its murky depths in neon flashes, like tiny shooting stars.

'Are you a boxing man Chris?' Barry asked, noticing me taking an interest in a cracked old photo of the Ali-Henry Cooper fight.

'Not really,' I admitted, 'I took up kick boxing a few years ago, but got the shit kicked out of me by an eleven year old, so that didn't last.' He gave the same gravelly chuckle I'd heard over the phone and sat down at his desk, a bikini-clad Britt Ekland framed on the wall behind him.

'Man With The Golden Gun?' I ventured.

'Well spotted mate!' he congratulated me. 'Limited edition, picked it up at a charity auction in London. You clearly know your Bond movies, Chris. Smoke?' Indicating a chair next to his own, he lit himself a cigarette and handed the pack and lighter to me. Leaning back in his big old recliner, 'So mate,' he said, 'what's your story?' effectively drawing the small talk portion of the afternoon to a close.

So I started telling him about Harrods and Louisa and her friends, and even the party, keeping out the bit about getting wasted obviously, as he smiled and nodded encouragement, occasionally chuckling quietly to himself. When I'd run out of things to say, considering I'd supplied the bare bones and covered them with a decent amount of flesh, he was still smiling.

'Good for you mate,' he congratulated me. 'Sounds like you've made a great link with this bird you've met in Harrods. A really good head start mate, you couldn't write it.'

'Do you think so Barry? Cheers.'

'I do. You've well and truly landed on your feet mate,' he continued. 'You do realise that's the elite, the top end, exactly what you were talking about getting into over the phone. So have you thrown the balls up her yet?'

'Thrown the balls up her?'

'Have you shagged her?' he clarified, with an indulgent grin. Now it was my turn to smile.

'No, I haven't Barry, I can't afford to, I'm saving every penny at the moment. And I'll be honest with you mate, I've never been with an escort,' I told him.

'Grow a pair mate,' he said, 'she's obviously keen on you, throw them up her, you lucky bugger!' His fingers drumming the desk, he took a second to compose his thoughts.

'I've got a good feeling about you Chris,' he finally said. 'I'm not gonna lie to yer mate, I was kind of expecting someone a bit older. You've still got a very young look to you, you know? How old are you Chris, if you don't mind me asking? Twenty-three? Twenty-four?'

'No, I just turned twenty-eight first of June.'

THE AGENCY

'Really? You look good for it mate,' he said, not sounding totally convinced. 'You know Chris, even at twenty-eight I think you're still gonna be one of the youngest agency owners in London? English-wise, for a bloke that is. Do you think you're ready for that?'

'What do you mean ready?' I asked him.

'Well, for the hard work mate. It's very long hours, a lot of web work with a content managed site. You're putting up all the photos and bios yourself. Then there's dealing with the punters, sorting the timewasters and the psychos. You'll have to learn on your feet, and quickly too. You're gonna have to start using your nut, mate.' He took a final drag from his cigarette, stubbed it out in a Caesar's Palace ashtray, and lit another. 'Look, let's not beat around the bush Chris, it's a tough business you're looking to get into,' he explained, 'especially at your age. It's not all plain sailing. But as I said, I have got a good feeling. Plus you know what Chris, it's really nice to see another English boy setting up an agency. It's been all Russians lately.'

This little pep talk over, we set to work on the site. And maybe because we'd bonded over Bond, or maybe because of the English connection, that afternoon at least it was all plain sailing. Barry really knew his stuff. He also seemed to know pretty much everyone in the business, and was responsible for designing probably a third of the really high-end agency sites.

He talked me through his work on some of the more exclusive ones, some of the sites that had caught my attention when I'd been researching from the man cave, using them to explain the features I'd need on my own site. 'You come from a retail background Chris, think of the homepage as your shop window,' he instructed, pulling the three monitors on his desk closer together, and working from all three at once. 'You need a classy colour scheme something like this, home page featured photos, here's a font I would recommend, and here's a stylish logo you could use.'

We'd blitzed the creative stuff in under an hour. By that time, I had a mocked-up homepage, with a black and platinum signature feel that just looked amazing, and we had a clear plan in place for the rest of the site. Barry had also committed to putting together an advertising package by our next meeting that he promised would 'definitely tick all the boxes.' I couldn't believe how much we'd accomplished in a single afternoon.

We were driving back through Southend, the day-trippers off the beach now and outside the early evening bars, pint glasses hovering over pink faces, when Barry broke a thoughtful silence. 'Mate, look,' he said, 'if you're gonna do this properly, there's a lot you're gonna need to know. Not the technical side of things, I'll look after that for you. But the business side.' He gave a furtive little look, the way people do when they're about to do something nice or unpleasant. 'I'm gonna put you in touch with a very good friend of mine who runs one of the big London agencies,' he said, I think he'd be a really useful contact,' and left it at that.

As the Range Rover climbed towards the station, I saw myself through Barry's eyes, a nice young lad who was a little innocent, a little out of his depth, but up for the challenge, and deserved a helping hand learning the ropes and getting started. I couldn't have been more grateful.

In Barry, and in Louisa, probably right at this moment winging her way back from some lucrative business trip, I couldn't really have found better or more supportive friends, and in what I'd have thought of just a few short weeks ago as the unlikeliest of places. When was all this good luck going to run out?

As the train into London sped past rolling hills and long summer shadows, there was that elusive happiness again. I was on my way.

# 4: It's all about who you know

Barry was as good as his word and arranged a meeting with his good mate Rob, an industry contact who just happened to be one of the kingpins of the London escorting scene. Running through the details over the phone, he'd also updated me on his own progress. My site could be up and running in as little as a couple of weeks, and now he told me I needed to put my money where my mouth was. Rob would explain the nuts and bolts of the business, or 'the nuts and the tits' as Barry had said, with a Sid James chuckle, but the rest was going to be up to me.

Barry had also let me know, and in no uncertain terms, exactly who I was dealing with in Rob, and that in meeting him I was diving straight in at the deep end of the pool. His was a top-drawer set up, the number one agency for high-end English girls. He had scores of elite escorts on his books, some of them even British porn stars and glamour models, and his clientele were the global money men: city boys, Harley Street consultants, top lawyers, and members of the rich list London drew like nowhere else. Louisa had opened the door, opened my eyes to this secret London with all its hidden wealth and trickle-down opportunity, but she couldn't show me how to grab it, make it mine the way Rob could. He'd been there, done that. He'd landed the golden ticket, and now he was offering to share what he'd learned along the way.

The great thing about this scenario was that Barry had already explained my situation, and the sort of agency I was looking to create, built on my connections with Louisa and her mostly Latina girlfriends. This meant there would be no overlap, no conflict of interest, and London's Mr. Big was more than happy to befriend and advise another English guy whose elite-end business wouldn't threaten his own, and might even rebalance national demographics a bit.

Rob had suggested meeting for lunch at the Royal Garden Hotel, at one end of High Street Ken, and within walking distance of Harrods. It was a hotel I was familiar with, from the outside at least, having passed it every day on the bus to and from work. It was still the sort of place I'd have been too intimidated to ever enter by myself though, one more London institution that reeked of privilege. From the street, its golden swirls and curlicues and top-hatted doormen served as a warning to keep a distance, and as you crossed its threshold you were surrounded by the identikit luxury that shone from a thousand business magazines. Its sleek, expensive interiors mimicked the first class business lounges I'd only ever glimpsed through a closing door, and imposed the same silent apartheid.

The funny thing was, breaching its defences in my Prada suit and pressed white shirt as I swept through its revolving glass doors, I was getting away with it, and passing for someone who belonged here. Suddenly I was on the other side of the counter, not serving but demanding to be served.

Rob was standing at the empty restaurant bar, chatting to an attentive barman under what must have been a thousand crystal chandelier, totally at home amidst the expensive sparkle. I guessed that, like Barry, he was mid to late forties. Immaculately groomed from head to toe, with a sharp haircut and George Hamilton tan, and his Saville Row suit tapering to a pair of gleaming Loakes, he looked in fact every inch the wealthy Harrods customer.

Introducing himself, he gripped my hand in a vigorous handshake, and then wrinkled back the sleeve of his jacket to consult a gold Rolex. 'Punctuality, mate, I like it,' he said, holding my eye with a steady, penetrating look so I wasn't sure whether he was trying to read me or intimidate me. 'If there's one thing I can't stand, it's people being late. Time's money,' he added, still not relaxing eye contact. It was a look that was actually quite difficult to handle, serious and dark-eyed, and I dropped my eyes to his hands. What was it with these guys and their Rolexes? And their tattoos apparently, a little scratch of blue just visible beneath his watch bracelet.

We were led over to a table on the far side of the restaurant with a view out over Kensington Palace Gardens, the park's top-heavy trees filling the picture window with their late summer froth. Behind them there was the faint sketch of a London skyline, and the imposing dome of the Royal Albert Hall. 'What do you fancy?' Rob asked, engaging in a cursory scan of the menu.

'What's good?' I deferred to his judgement. He seemed to know the hotel inside out after all, from the barman to the manager, and they all seemed to know him too, coming over every so often to welcome him by name as though he owned the place. 'Mate, everything's good here' he grinned, clearly in his element and enjoying his status.

The restaurant was one of those places that, even when full, would still have felt empty, the discreetly spaced tables with their starched white cloths like scattered sailboats on a still lake. The entire room seemed to be holding a hushed breath, just the tinkling of a piano somewhere, and restrained conversations rising in a jumble of languages. It supplied one of those strange moments of clarity: this was what money bought you in this city, what wealth provided: unobtrusive luxury shared only with the similarly wealthy, all the rough edges and nasty surprises of life folded away.

I followed Rob's lead, and we ordered like a pair of true

carnivores, twin rump steaks and a bottle of red that he was particularly partial to. Rob got straight down to business. 'So Chris, Barry gave me the heads up. I understand you've made a really good link in Harrods, you lucky sod. He sent me the details of Amanda's site. What a stunner! And what a Bill Oddie! If the other girls she's introducing you to look anything like her, you're on to a real winner! Christ', he laughed, sliding back in his chair, 'I understand it was a bit of a shock when she told you she was a brass.'

'Brass?'

'Brass nail. Tail. It's the rhyming slang for prossie mate,' he explained.

'To be honest with you Rob,' I admitted, 'I wasn't even sure what Amanda meant when she told me she was an escort.'

He laughed appreciatively, and a little loudly for this place, though the surfeit of noise disappeared almost instantly, absorbed in the room's acoustics. A room designed, I guessed, for turning a deaf ear. 'Barry told me you don't have a great deal of money to get the ball rolling,' he ran on diplomatically, 'but it sounds like you could potentially have a nice selection of high class girls. I'm sure those girls are gonna generate a lot of interest.'

This was such a strange conversation to be having, particularly in this setting. I'd spent the last few weeks imagining this world of escorts, agencies and owners, and here it suddenly was, being served up to me over lunch in an exclusive London hotel as though it was a perfectly normal way in the world to spend an afternoon. 'You're a bit of a lad, aren't you, to get in to all of this! I love it!' he grinned, stabbing at a forkful of green salad. 'Elite Latin birds are highly sought-after.'

'I've only met Amanda and her flatmate so far,' I admitted, 'and they're lovely, but this is all very new to me, I'm still trying to take it all in. To be honest, I can't really believe this is happening.' He scanned me in my Prada suit as though he was taking me in for the first time, and a corner of his mouth twitched in something like amusement. 'You're a very charming, very polite young man,' he said. 'Well I'm a proud Londoner, a Wembley boy at heart,' I countered, 'but Harrods does rub off on you, and you do pick up a few airs and graces I suppose.' I didn't want to totally dispel the illusion.

'That's really gonna help you mate,' Rob smiled, 'you're gonna be dealing with a lot of wealthy, high-end clients. These guys are CEOs, businessmen, serious money, they're used to getting the best of everything, and that's what you will need to convey. But I'm sure you won't have a problem, considering your background. It's all a big old confidence trick at heart, mate.'

I watched him hesitate, holding back his next thought while the waiter unobtrusively removed our salad plates and replaced them with the two rump steaks, the smell of seared meat rising over the table like a thermal current. 'I don't know how much Barry told you about my setup,' he resumed, one eye still on the retreating waiter, 'but I only started with a handful of girls, what was it –around five years ago. God, time's flown. If I'd had the start you're having, with Barry building your site, getting an introduction to someone like me, and meeting a total sort like Amanda, things would have been a lot easier. Anyway, now I have two full-time receptionists, and an admin girl who looks after the website and all the advertising. Cost me a fortune but they're worth every penny. When this quality of client calls to make a booking, they definitely don't want to hear some Essex wide boy like me at the other end of the line. You on the other hand, a Harrods boy, they'll lap it up. You sound like the fucking maître d' of this place, who's actually a very nice bloke. Always makes me laugh coming here, these posh sods running around after me.'

He smiled, and tipped back the bulb of his wine glass with evident satisfaction. 'But running an agency isn't just dealing with clients and setting up bookings,' he continued, 'it takes a certain skillset. You have to understand mate, these are not normal birds you're going to be working with. They can be a right mixed bag. Some are real business women, very professional, sex is literally meaningless to them; others are genuine nymphomaniacs, can't get enough of it; a few can be a bit highly strung, get a bit emotional from time to time. You may become a bit of a therapist to these girls, even if half of them are in therapy already. They're gonna want to open up to you, you're gonna be their first port of call, and sometimes it may get a bit heavy.'

Louisa flashed into my mind, probably in her South Ken apartment right now, possibly with a client even, while we were here working on our steaks. In the short time I'd known her, talked to her, planned with her and fantasised about her, did I really know anything about what made her tick, *the sort of bird she really was*, as Rob might say? 'What it boils down to, Rob continued, 'is whatever they're like, respect them, be nice, don't be an arsehole. After all, you're gonna make a lot of money together. But one thing I must advise you, is keep well away from any girl with a Roger Rabbit.'

I was struggling to hold back a little smile. Here I was, with a powerhouse of London escorting, which was all Alice in Wonderland enough, and now we were talking cartoon characters. He registered my confusion with an indulgent chuckle, and tapped his index finger against one side of his nose. 'Roger Rabbit. Habit.'

'Sorry Rob' I smirked, 'I was born in Wembley, not Bethnal Green. Apples and pears, dog and bone I understand but that's about it when it comes to rhyming slang.'

'Don't worry, you'll pick it up in time,' he beamed back.

Between Louisa's friends with their broken English, and Barry and Rob, it felt like I was being linguistically assaulted from all sides.

'Girls with a habit, you're not going to be able to rely on them,' Rob explained.

'Some clients want to experience 'altered states of perception' with a girl, if you get my meaning, do a few lines or have a drink. There are girls who can handle it, but a lot who can't.' I thought back to the party, the lines of coke, the glass table crowded with booze, and the ecstasy tablets handily stashed in the console. 'Some clients, particularly the old city boys, will even ask if you can supply it. Keep well away from that carry on. *That's* where you're gonna get yourself into trouble'

I could see a pattern now to Rob's advice. Always the same emphatic certainty, never any room for doubt or debate. He clearly understood the industry and was in complete control of his response to it. 'Look Chris,' he continued, 'I'm not gonna be able to give you all the pointers to running an agency over a single lunch, but I take it you've done some research. The vast majority of bookings are in calls, obviously that's when the punter visits the brass. But you're also going to be setting up a lot of out calls all over London, or even further afield, the home counties, all over the UK and even internationally. The girls' availability is the key here. Some work every day and every hour God sends, others will only work the odd day. They set their hours, you have to go along with it. On any given day I can have anything from sixty to a hundred girls available, all expecting work. But my girls mess me around all the time, have three hour hair appointments, or disappear to the gym for half the fuckin' day, and still give me a hard time for not getting them enough work. But that's the way it goes, and there's no point falling out with them, you'll get used to it.'

'What about when I'm on the phone to the clients?' I asked him.

'It's easy. You want to turn the call around quick, a few key questions, keep it short and sweet. All you wanna know is who they wanna see, what time, how long for, in call or out call, confirm the fee and that's pretty much it. The quicker you're contacting the escort and offering her the booking, the quicker you can get back to the client and put it all to bed. It will be slow to start,' he warned, 'but it will pick up. And at least you're gonna be up and running this side of Christmas. You'll see what Christmas is like with the office parties and all the fun and games that come with that. You'll have a good Christmas, I'll guarantee it Chris,' he joked 'It's gonna be manic.'

'That's exactly what Amanda said,' I laughed. 'I'm just worried about the risks of starting something like this.'

'What fuckin' risks?' he shot back defiantly. 'Listen fella, relax, all you're doing is setting up bookings on the girls' behalf. Think of it as an introduction service. Obviously there are some grey areas, but the authorities are the least of your worries, they don't give a monkeys. The law have got their hands full with the cheap end of the market, those scumbags trafficking birds in.'

'Yeah I guess, but what about the competition?' I asked him.

'Competition is healthy,' Rob replied. 'In fact, some my former girls retired out of the game and set up their own agencies. And good luck to them. There's enough work out there for all of us. It's an unbelievably lucrative business if you get it right.'

Rob consulted his Rolex. 'Listen fella,' he said, lowering his voice a notch, 'another thing, no more Chris. In our line of work you need to stay under the radar. People will wonder who you are, they will naturally gossip. You're gonna have to dream up a whole new persona, a whole new identity. Nobody uses their real name in this business. My name's not Rob, obviously. I've forgotten my real name,' he laughed. 'You got any ideas?' I looked out through the picture window, running through the sorts of names that might fit the bill.

'What do you think of Tony?' I asked him.

'Yeah, that's fine. It'll be easy for the girls and the clients to remember. What made you think of that?'

'I watched back to back Sopranos last night.'

## THE AGENCY

'Ah, Tony Soprano, what a legend! A man after my own heart,' he laughed. 'Listen Chris, or should I say Tony? I know it's a lot to take in, and you've still got loads to learn, but you seem like a really good lad. You'll be alright.' And all it took was those few words from Rob for the agency to suddenly become real.

When the bill came, Rob's hand beat mine to the little leather folder, and he slid it to his side of the table, chucking his credit card inside without bothering to consult the bill. 'I'd like to pay, if you don't mind,' I feebly protested.

'Don't be silly mate, you're gonna need every penny you've got, you've got some serious overheads to come,' he laughed. 'And listen, before I forget, I've got one golden rule for you before I go. Whatever you do, don't fall for one of these girls. Don't get yourself emotionally connected. I do appreciate easier said than done. After all, you're bound to mix business with pleasure, that's the name of the game, but just bear it in mind. Right, sorry mate, I've got to shoot off,' he said, reaching for his mobile to call his driver.

As we were making our way out of the restaurant, he asked me about my friends and my family, and what they thought of it all. I told him I didn't have much family left, only an elderly Aunt Violet in North London, and I wouldn't be rushing to tell her about this any time soon. And as for my mates, I honestly wasn't sure how they were going to react, they were all quite settled, some with girlfriends, some with wives and kids already. 'Bollocks to anybody's opinion!' he said, in a sudden display of emotion. 'At the end of the day you're not going to be doing anything wrong. But you just wait and see mate, in time some of your mates will become your number one fans. Any red-blooded male is going to be intrigued. They'll be begging to know all about it.'

As his driver pulled up in front of the hotel, he took my hand in another vice-like grip. 'Sure I can't drop you anywhere?' he asked. I thanked him anyway, but told him I was going to have a crafty cigarette before heading home. 'Ok mate, you've got my number,' he said, 'call me anytime. Now be lucky fella.' And with that, he disappeared into the Merc's dark leather interior.

# 5: Jumping ship

I stood on the hotel steps watching Rob's Mercedes slip into an expensive jam of traffic building its own heat shimmer, and allowing myself a few long, deep breaths. Once I was a bit calmer, I started thinking back over everything that had just happened, to see if it might feel any more real the second time around.

    I'd just spent the best part of a two hour lunch with a major player, one of London's top agency owners, and he had as much as said I was up to competing in the big leagues, maybe even building a premiership outfit. He'd told me I had the character and the charm, for want of a better word, to make it all happen. I was totally tripping out on this high-octane meeting with Rob, his vote of confidence and the two bottles of red spreading a nervy elation through my entire body.

    Pacing back and forth in front of the hotel smoking a shaky cigarette, I replayed the events of the lunch, trying to remember as much of Rob's advice as I could. I was cursing myself now for not having taken notes or made some sort of recording, though I doubted the request would have gone down too well. I took my phone and instinctively scrolled to Louisa's number, picturing her mobile coming to life in the cool South Ken apartment.

There was a disheartening sequence of rings before Louisa's voice spilled out with its own seductive music, and my body instinctively unwound another loop, then tied itself up all over again. Balancing the mobile between my ear and shoulder, I grabbed and lit another cigarette to calm my nerves, and listened to myself tripping over my words in my hurry to tell her all about the lunch. I wasn't making a whole lot of sense as I tried to retell the story while still coming to terms with it. Not that it mattered. Louisa was already laughing contagiously at my excitement, telling me to calm down, she was at home, and I should come over to explain the good news in person, whatever it was.

So I set off in the direction of her apartment still spilling sweaty energy. The afternoon heat had hit me like a wall the moment I'd stepped out of the air-conditioned hotel. I could already feel little trickles of sweat creeping under my shirt collar and down my back like an army of tiny, slow-moving insects. As I left High Street Ken, and started racing along the back roads towards South Kensington, I was already onto another cigarette, still tightly wound, and I knew I'd be chain smoking all the way to Louisa's door.

The grand Georgian streets stretched out in front of me

like a flatter, broader version of the rest of London, school parties straggling in lines under their looming turrets and spires. The kids looked punch drunk in the late afternoon heat, probably still on a high from the Natural History Museum and its towering piles of dinosaur bones. Ducking in and out of the narrow strips of shade hanging at the streets' edges, I must have looked pretty punch drunk myself: some sweaty, chain smoking lunatic, weaving past random tourists in my rush to get to Louisa's, and make sense of everything that had just happened with Rob.

So many conflicting thoughts were playing through my head. How thinking back on meeting Rob already seemed surreal, and yet had made everything more real, had brought me within touching distance of opening my own agency. And how I now urgently needed to talk to Louisa's friends and get them on board. Just talking to Rob I'd felt the doors of this secret world opening up to me, with all their Masonic rules, their codes of conduct and time-honoured laws. There had of course been that tacit menace of Rob's stare, but his offer of help had felt so generous and genuine, and he seemed so comfortable in that world, did I really have anything to fear from it?

And now I was racing to Louisa's. Mesmerising Louisa, the fulcrum of this whole venture. Rob might assume she was just one more brass to treat with respect but keep at a distance, but from what I could see she and Rob weren't so very different. They might be from different sides of the business, but they shared the same focus, understood the system and how you used it rather than let it use you.

I was the one still with this vague uneasiness I was being drawn into a world I didn't fully understand, and should probably leave well alone, even as I was committing myself to it. What was it about me that was still holding me back? I was walking past the Natural History Museum and the V & A, their Millennia of fact and opinion all mixed up, part of a world constantly shifting and reforming. Was anyone ever really convinced of anything? Were Rob and Louisa really any more certain than I was? Or was it just that old confidence trick Rob had talked about? Should I just accept there would always be things I couldn't control and, like Rob and Louisa, go with the flow?

I'd been brought up to do the right thing, work hard and avoid unnecessary risks. But 'no risk, no reward,' as Rob and Barry would say. The rules were different in this new world, everyone knew that. The wealthy and successful looked after their own. Money inoculated you, protected you, encouraged others to turn a deaf ear, and fuck everyone else. Rob's confidence, the way he owned a room, the way Louisa drew the world and the Harrods rooftop to her, they were so seductive. I wanted that too. Along, of course, with the

Rolexes, the chauffeur driven cars and the luxury apartments. And right on cue, I found myself standing outside Louisa's.

Her voice floated for a second on the electric crackle of the intercom, followed by a faint buzz and the click of a latch. By the time I'd reached her apartment, the door already stood open. This was the first time I'd been here since the night of the party, the night that had set me on my current course, and the contrast hit me. No Samba beat. No sea of bodies. Just perfect stillness, the whir of the air conditioning system and the white noise of London scorching the silence. At that moment she appeared from behind the French windows, their hazy rectangle of late afternoon light shifting around her as she walked towards me, making a halo of her dark hair, and streaming around her curves.

Louisa. Always with the ability to surprise. Smaller, somehow, in the blown open apartment, and even more beautiful. She squeezed me to her, kissed me on each cheek, and invited me on to the balcony. Following her, I realised she was beautiful in a way I could never quite create in my mind's eye, even when I was fantasising about her. This must be the most casual I had ever seen her. Not Chanel-suited for Harrods, not the fantasy men paid for. Just in cut-off shorts and a cotton vest, and she'd never looked sexier. For weeks I'd tried to lock away my feelings for her, occupying myself with the agency. In a split second she had sprung the lock, and all the heat and confusion came pressing down on me.

Stepping onto the balcony, there was a rush of memory from the night of the party. The two of us together here on ecstasy, our reeling conversation and the rush of the night sky with its swell of emotion (retreating surf and crashing wave). Helplessly, I watched her open the bottle of wine that had been set out on the table next to a couple of oversized glasses.

'Are you trying to get me even more drunk?' I joked nervously, 'I've already shared a couple of bottles over lunch. You might have noticed I'm a little bit tipsy.' She looked at me curiously, and laughed. It was oppressively hot; the stored-up heat of the afternoon and the long Indian summer. Up close, I could feel the heat radiating from her, moistening the glittery sheen of her skin. 'Chris, we're celebrating, remember?' she said, tipping the bottle, and the wine leaping into my glass like a bolt of electricity on the slow current of the afternoon.

We lit a couple of cigarettes, and sucked up the mellow heat. And suddenly all I could feel was heat. The heat of the day. The twisting heat of the cigarette. Heat in my face and body. Could she sense it, hear my heart thumping? This was the first time we'd been completely by ourselves, and this aloneness carried its own dangerous momentum. A summer afternoon, and the threat of a thunderstorm lurking at its margins.

I started telling her about the meeting with Rob, talking

rapidly, worried my voice would betray me. Louisa had heard of his agency. 'It's very well known,' she said, 'I know a couple of girls who have worked with them. They're always so busy. It's a pity they only work with English girls.'

I watched as she ran her fingers along the stem of the wine glass. When she laughed there was that same ecstatic surge, that same serotonin kick I'd felt on the night of the party. I wondered what would happen if, right now, I leant across the table, and drew her mouth to mine? She would surely pull away. Wouldn't she? Not that I would ever have the courage to find out. At some point I was going to leave her here in this apartment, a perfect jewel in its perfect casing. Life was going to resume, and I going to get on with the serious business of building an agency. I recognised the fact with a mix of excitement and faint anxiety. 'Anyway,' I said, 'he was a very cool dude, really looked the part. Plus he was a wealth of information. It was great to get to meet a big time agency owner.'

I heard myself telling her my own site would be up and running in less than a month, and that I would now need her help contacting her friends to see who was interested in joining, watching her eyes widen as she caught hold of the implications. 'Oh my god' she said dramatically, 'it's all happening so quickly.'

'How many girls do you think will be interested?' I asked her, thinking back to Rob and his story of starting up his agency with only a handful. 'Chris, honestly, I can already think of at least fifteen,' she said, 'and maybe more than that in time.' I was discussing the practicalities of my agency with a high class escort I couldn't stop thinking about.... but so long as I kept talking...

'You know what else Rob told me to do?' I ran on, 'I've had to dream up a new name. No more Chris'

'Of course, we all do, you're talking to Amanda remember,' she replied, smiling mischievously. 'What name are you thinking?'

'What do you think of Tony? He's a mafia boss on a television show,' I laughed.

'Chris I like it,' she said, 'Tony. Antonio. My friends will love that. Ok Tony,' she tried it out again for size, 'no more Chris and Louisa. From now on we're Tony and Amanda. Less confusion.'

She clapped her hands delightedly. A new name for a new business. It was a milestone, a new beginning. I wasn't Chris any more, the lonely guy on the Harrods roof terrace who had loved Louisa from a distance while the world revolved on its axis. Now I was Tony, quaffing wine on a South Ken balcony with this beautiful woman, almost literally on top of the world, and more than a little pissed.

'So how are we going to celebrate, Tony?' Amanda asked,

glancing back over her shoulder into the dim, empty apartment. There was a heady, crashing silence, before she met her question with another question. 'You want to fuck?' she asked, her words cutting through the heavy afternoon like the promised storm, obliterating the London skyline, washing doubt away. Not waiting for an answer, she took my hand and led me back into the apartment.

\*

I watched Amanda light a second cigarette as I made my way back to her bed, calmly taking in the fact of her newly revealed nakedness, and enjoying how her body emitted its own dusky glow in the dusky light. Honey. Amber. Burnished gold. Everything that only an hour before had been the focus of desperate hopes and hopeless anxieties, now instantly and oddly familiar. How completely something could change in a split second of thunder. But then if knowing Amanda these last months had taught me anything, it was surely that. I quickly got back into bed beside her, an uncertain buffer against the night and finding myself out in it.

When Amanda had taken my hand and led me away from the balcony, all the want slowly stacking up not only that afternoon, but in all the weeks leading up to it, had crashed against a sudden doubt. For a moment I'd resisted, stupidly stuttered something about not having the money. Knowing, even if I had, paying like just another client would have betrayed something in me: my pride, the grander scale of whatever these feelings were that had been at play. 'Don't be silly,' she had said in her offhand way, unoffended. 'It's how do you English say, on the house.'

And from there she had taken control, had led me into the quiet apartment and down the dimly lit hallway, the same steps I'd taken on the night of the party, but now filled with her guiding silhouette and her citrusy perfume on the sway of her long dark hair. And then there had been that bedroom, only glimpsed on the night of the party with its unbroken line of mirrors, and that great fantasy of a bed. The most luxurious bed you could ever fuck on, I'd thought back then, like a giant sensual cloud.

She had pushed me back into its firm bounce, and slowly undressed me and then herself, unbuckling, unbuttoning, tugging at sleeves and hems. Stepping back, she had pulled her vest up over her incredible boobs and slid out of her shorts and panties, with a minimum of fuss, but still I'd noticed with a sense of prideful performance. Finally she had been standing smoothly naked in front of me, her clothes tumbled with mine at her feet.

I had felt the charge of her body, those full breasts with their brown areole and hard nipples, and breathed in the fleshier scents her confined nakedness had released. Watching her spin around to show off a sweep of hair that fell almost to her full Latina bum, I had been aware of her sense of her own worth, a woman for whom every intimacy was also a showing and a validation.

Leading me into her shower, she had pressed my hands against the undercurve of her breasts as the water fell down between us in a fine spray, beading on her shoulders, and pooling and tumbling in little rivers over her smooth skin, creating a slick between my body and hers. She had squeezed shower gel into one hand, instantly releasing a flood of exotic scents, then worked the lather gently into my chest and then my back in wide sweeps, pressing the slipperiness of her body against me to the contrast of white and gold, and finally lowering her reach to tease my bum.

Then she had been kneeling in front of me, slowly lathering and then rinsing my dick, then taking it into her mouth with a kind of tender ritual. Her mouth had produced a startling depth of pleasure that left me gasping, my heavy breaths masked in the noises of falling water, and my dick so hard that as she released it, it sprang violently upwards. It had only been a couple of months ago I had been too scared to even talk to Louisa, and now here I was looking down at this beautiful woman giving me the most intense pleasure I could recall. I smiled down at her, and she slowly rose to her feet, reached for a bath towel and wrapped us both in it. It was like being wrapped in furs.

And then we were back in the bedroom, and kissing for the first time, an explosion of a kiss, all mouths and tongues and heat and chaos. She gently pushed me back onto the bed, then was above me and on me again, her lips locked to mine, her damp hair falling like a curtain, and tickling my neck. Eyes connecting for a second. A flash of glistening boob. A hot mouth wet against a nipple. Then her lips on my stomach, teeth pulling on thick hair, her mouth lowered around my dick, and her hand expertly gripping and her wrist twisting. She reached over to a bedside cabinet, ripped open a metallic square, and slid a condom onto my dick, using her lips and the sliding pressure of her mouth to unroll it along the length of my shaft.

And then, as I lay there, she straddled me, my hands reaching up to her waist and a tremor rising through me, as I forced my back into a convex arch. She leaned forwards so my head was between her breasts, the scent of the shower gel all mixed up with the taste and slick of her skin, as she rhythmically rode me, slowly and repeatedly falling onto me. We were suddenly into a rhythm, her fingers in my hair, my hands controlling her movements, and I was losing myself in the dim half-light of passion, feeling the release, the heady joyfulness of the fuck.

But Amanda was already changing tack. She had pushed herself up, and was now prostrated on the bed, wanting, it seemed, to give me her full VIP experience, show me everything that she knew, everything she had learned. I had stepped back from the bed to take in the contours of her body, its generosity and firmness. Kneeling behind her, I pulled the fullness of her incredible Brazilian arse to me, and thrust into her, arching over her as I did it to taste the dewy curve of her back. I glanced over to the wall of mirrors where this thrusting image was reflected, watching my hands reaching around her to cup her boobs. I was forcing myself deeper into her now, pure Tony, as her back arched against me, not resisting but yielding. There was a rising tension as I drove harder into her. Edging close, I gave up to the sensation, pumping, filling her, and finally falling depleted onto the bed, our mixed up breaths slowly quieting. I was barely aware now of her dexterously sliding off the spent condom, and caressing my softening dick. Then she kissed me, softly and briskly on the lips, sealing the deal, and silently offered me a cigarette.

'So what did Tony think of Amanda?' she'd asked, as I caught my breath in the twilight, my eyes stinging with sweat as I watched her taking the first drag of her cigarette.

'He really enjoyed it, that was amazing,' I stuttered, still absorbing what had just happened.

'Good, me too,' she replied. Nothing more.

Later, we'd fucked a second time. Amanda had initiated again, her kisses falling on my ears and neck, her tongue licking and teasing as her hands and mouth slowly travelled south across and along my body in sensual zigzags. But this time I'd asserted myself, catching hold of her lithe, small body and twisting her around and on to her back, my weight over her. This time she offered no resistance as my fingers played between her legs, and as I lifted her to my mouth and tasted the deep wet heat. Then, pressing my weight down onto her, I probed at first almost ponderously, feeling the way our bodies locked together, then more recklessly, while she moaned and whispered unknown phrases, and my body dictated to hers. I was holding on to every detail, the rolling of her breasts, her glistening skin, her heavy, irregular breaths, as I lost myself. There was a rush of fire, inevitable heat and burn, a shudder, a synchronicity. And maybe it fools you, as you lock eyes and bodies, soaked in the same sweat and the same heat, but that sense of a moment that promises its own traction.

And now in the calm dusk I was lying with this beautiful woman, thinking no doubt as her clients did that I was crazy not to be fucking her again, feeling all of her, but enjoying the quiet intimacy of the moment, and wanting nothing else. I was thinking back to Rob's injunction to caution when Amanda kissed me lightly on the lips. 'You're a good fuck,' I heard her say in the darkness, 'you made me come. Most guys have no idea.'

But I was lost in the moment, and lost in Amanda, the perfect woman, the loyal friend, the escort men paid to fuck.

It was already dark when I left Amanda's. However much I'd wanted to stay, I instinctively knew that wasn't what this was. We'd drunk wine and laughed and fucked and smoked and felt something. The only promise we'd made to each other was that the next day she would sound out her friends about my agency, and I would finally take the leap and hand in my Harrods notice.

And I was as good as my word, dropping my resignation letter into HR the very next day. The manager there had scanned the letter that was clearly set to ruin her morning, then poked and prodded for any sign I'd cave and retract, but sniffing out my certainty had flashed a defeated smile and, to round things off, asked me about my plans. To keep things simple, I'd told her I was off travelling.

'Anywhere nice?' she'd asked. I'd thought on my feet.

'Through South America,' Tony shot back with a winning smile.

I was well and truly jumping ship.

# 6: Learning the ropes

So here I was, counting down the days to this new life, and if my Harrods focus was waning by the hour, I was applying myself to my new business with the mindset of a Jedi. Evenings and days off I'd be in my cramped man cave, hunched over my trusty Dell, and smoking like a trooper as day became night and then became day again.   Occasionally an email would land in my inbox that wasn't more of the porn avalanche my web searches were clearly triggering: pay-per-view voyeur sites, and ads for Herbal Viagara that promised to make a new man of me, even as they got in the way of me making a new man of myself. There were a trickle of technical ones from Barry, that could have been written in Sanskrit for all I understood of them, and then a distracting flurry of applications from Amanda's friends, the girls who were going to make or break me.

    Erica was the first to get in touch, a Mexican beauty based in Paddington with a dark mane of hair that tumbled to her waist, and a starting hourly rate of five hundred pounds. Then Bella, a petite Brazilian with the cutest smile, who worked out of Mayfair and charged a minimum six hundred. Where did she score those extra hundred pounds? Something she'd talk me through, no doubt, or Amanda or Rob next time I saw them. Pricing was something I had still spectacularly failed to get my head around: why girls who looked so similarly perfect advertised at such different rates.

Then there was Nicole, Brazilian and with an apartment right next door to Liverpool Street. Only twenty-one but with a poise and sophistication, in her photos at least, that belied her youth. I wondered just what those beautiful green eyes had seen that allowed them to meet the camera with such mesmerising equanimity. And Denise, at twenty-five, what were the events in her life that had propelled her all the way from Buenos Aires to a penthouse in Baker Street? So many journeys, so many stories, and not all of them fairy tales, I was sure of that.

By the week's end I'd been messaged by a dozen girls, some with English so broken that deciphering their emails was like cracking code, others who wrote with the detached polish of MBA applicants, some just chatty and friendly and reminding me of Amanda.

It was strange to think that all these girls, from home towns and cities scattered across the plains and mountain ranges of South and Central America, and sharing nothing more than the common currency of beauty, had all been drawn to a few square miles of prime London real estate by global economics and the whispered promise of a better life.

All the girls had attached between five and ten photos to their applications and, one by one, they shimmied on my monitor draped in lingerie in expensive-looking studios, and in tiny bikinis on empty, exclusive-looking beaches. Some had attached more informal photos taken in their own apartments. One had included a shot of herself on horseback, a mountain range soaring in the background. Another was posing demurely in front of what I thought I recognised as the Taj Mahal. One of the Brazilian girls had sent a picture of herself in hiking boots, looking down on the ruins of Machu Picchu.

I tried to second-guess the stories behind these photos. Had the girl at the Taj Mahal been on a 'business trip' with a wealthy Indian client? Had he taken the photo on his camera and mailed it to her, and did he keep a copy on a computer somewhere, hidden from a wife and children? Had the Machu Picchu girl been trekking with friends on some sort of gap year? I doubted a client would pay for an escort to accompany him on a hiking expedition, however stunning she and the scenery might be, and she could probably earn enough from a month's escorting in London to pay for a year of these sorts of life-changing experiences most people only dreamed of. Whatever you thought of the choices these girls were making, the world certainly opened itself up to them, the gift of superior genes its own blank cheque, if you were willing to cash it.

The last application to land in my inbox was from Amanda's flatmate Giselle, the girl in the cut down shorts and t-shirt who had been so friendly on the night of the party. It seemed a bit lax of her to be bringing up the rear, when I guessed she must have been one of the first girls Amanda had told, but then I wasn't about to hold that against her. She had set out a fairly lengthy biography, and attached a model comp card and a few other photos that had clearly been taken in the South Ken apartment. The comp card featured two modelling shoots, one of her in designer swimwear on a picture postcard beach, and the other a lingerie ad for a boutique fashion label I'd heard of, three intertwined, scantily clad models, with her in the middle, coolly impassive.

It was a bit of a shock to realise she was making a go of modelling in London, and still escorting, but I suppose it really shouldn't have been. In all these photos she was the same stunning girl I remembered from the night of the party, not as curvy as Amanda, but tall and rangy, a perfect model look. I could see her totally owning London fashion week, prowling the catwalk by day, and by night making a killing from the well-heeled hangers-on it always drew.

From the little I knew about the modelling world, escorting had to be the more lucrative option. Harrods was full of beautiful girls signed to model agencies, and competition amongst them was intense, not just for the big campaigns, but even for the unpaid shoots with edgy designers and photographers there was that outside chance might launch a career.

Giselle's comp card gave her age, height and measurements (the vital statistics of leery Miss World days), then in her email she'd set down her list of conditions. 'I do not see clients over sixty years of age, and my face must be blurred with all my images,' she had written. She'd also listed the services she offered. Making sense of these was proving something of a challenge. Some, like dinner dates and spanking, were pretty self-explanatory but I got stuck on most of the acronyms. What was GFE? I Googled it, but Good Faith Estimate seemed a bit of a stretch. And A levels? I was guessing it had nothing to do with her achievements in the classroom, even if most of these girls had stacks more academic qualifications than I ever would.

\*

I'd arranged to meet Amanda later that week for a lunchtime catch-up on the roof terrace. She'd been on my mind since that afternoon at her apartment, but life had got in the way since then, and I hadn't contacted her to talk about what had happened and she hadn't contacted me. Now, with only seventeen working days left at Harrods, it hit me as I bounded up the grand staircase there wouldn't be too many more of these shared panoramic lunches for us to enjoy.

When I got out onto the roof terrace she was there waiting on the other side of the glass doors, back in her trademark Chanel, a cigarette already in her hand, and I was left catching my breath, and not only from my uphill sprint. Amanda was in the building, and I was almost dizzy with this newest secret that hovered between us.

We hugged, and she kissed me on both cheeks, then fumbled through her Chanel bag for a tissue and wiped away the smeary evidence. Just her touch had taken me back to that afternoon at her apartment, but steering clear of what was starting to feel like a taboo, I told her instead about handing in my notice, and thanked her for keeping her side of our bargain and spreading the word amongst her friends.

'Of course, they're all absolutely stunning,' I said, still a little breathless, still a little guarded. 'It's just hit me now that's everything's changing. I have no idea what's about to happen, where I'm going to end up.'

'Who does?' she laughed, twisting her luscious lips, and giving nothing away. 'Don't worry, you'll be fine.'

In the last couple of days the Indian summer London had been enjoying had come to an abrupt end. The blue skies that had started to feel like an unchanging backdrop to our lunchtime confidences had given way to grey, knotted clouds and when the sun did fitfully break through, it was without any real authority. The change chimed with a sense of something coming to an end. Next week it would be October, and fewer of the Harrods crew would be coming up to the terrace in their lunch hours; we'd soon be down to the hard-core bronchial cases, as smokers were forced to weigh their addiction against the biting cold, sheltering behind these very glass doors. But then, thank God for nicotine cravings. Without them, Amanda and I wouldn't be here together right now.

The abrupt shift had set me thinking back to the previous winter, and the couple of weeks when London had been practically snowbound, blankets of the white stuff falling in gusts and swirls and eddies, and building a drifting city of snow, black cabs and red buses churning through the slush. From up here you got to see London in flux, rotating through all its seasons, as it absorbed the dreams of the newly arrived and discarded those of everyone who had fallen out of love with the city. Amanda and her friends were just a few handfuls among the thousands. I thanked her for rallying these new arrivals.

'So how do you know all these girls?' I asked her. Given the time I'd spent reading their biographies and looking over their pictures, I felt I could hazard some sort of guess at their backgrounds and the journeys they'd made. Some would be big city girls who'd grown into an awareness of their power over men early; some, girls from the country who had won beauty pageants, been signed by agents, and come to it all raw. They had probably met people at castings, or in bars and clubs, people who knew people, and somewhere along the line been inducted into this loop of self-assured beauties flying back and forth between Rio, Caracas and London.

'Oh you know, from home and through work,' she answered, hardly answering at all.

'Not really,' I nudged her, genuinely interested. She gave a resigned sigh, clearly deciding on explanation as the path of least resistance. 'Sometimes you arrive at a booking Tony,' she said, 'and there will already be five or six girls there.'

'Like an orgy, you mean?'

'You could say that,' she smiled. 'And at points in the evening you go to the bathroom together with another girl, get talking, maybe share a cab home if you're heading in the same direction, and if you've worked well together then you swap numbers.'

'And why do all these girls choose London?' I asked her.

'Same reason as me,' she said. 'Opportunity. Sex is like breathing, in Brazil at least. It's who we are. And money and sex live side by side in London. You English have more hang ups, but we do our best to change that.'

'So if you hadn't come here, what would you be doing now?' I asked her. She paused, considering. 'I'd be working in a department store in my home town maybe, saving for a little house, maybe married, maybe with a kid. Struggling.'

'But aren't there things about home you miss?'

'Why would I stay in Brazil?' she shot back, a note of challenge in her voice. 'It's not like London, all the money, all the possibility. It's another mentality. Look, you can't really describe it to someone who isn't from where I'm from. You're born poor, you stay poor. These are things you can't change. Here, you can do anything. Anyway,' she said, now closing down the discussion, 'I have two girlfriends coming from my hometown next week, who I know will want to join you straight away. Perhaps you can ask *them* why they're here.'

'Thanks, I'd planned to start meeting some of your friends next week anyway,' I told her, 'but there are things in their applications I really don't get. Giselle mentioned she does GFE, for example. What's that?'

'Not here!' Amanda hissed, her eyes widening in admonition, even as her serious voice collapsed into an amused giggle. 'This absolutely isn't a conversation for Harrods. Call me when you get home, any time before nine. We really need to work on your escorting education Tony!'

\*

When I got home I emptied a Whiskas pouch for Bubbles and got straight on the phone to Amanda. 'Tony, I've got twenty minutes,' she cut into my greeting, 'then I have to make myself beautiful.'

'Ok, so let's get to it,' I said, acknowledging a twisting envy for the lucky client she'd be buzzing up to her apartment later, as I reached for my notebook. 'Question number one.....and by the way Amanda, you're never not beautiful.'

'Tony, sooo sweet!' she purred. 'That's why you're a great agent!' We both laughed at her premature launching of my new career.

'Ok. So I'm trying to understand why these girls, who are all equally stunning, charge such different rates.'

'Tony, the girls decide what they want to earn, based on their looks, their education, their location, and the services they offer,' she replied. I had Giselle's application on my screen, and she had a sliding scale of fees linked to acronyms I could make neither head nor tail of. 'So what is GFE?' I asked, starting at the top.

'Ok, so that's easy. Girlfriend experience.'

'Which means what? Arguing over who gets to hog the remote?'

'More like a fantasy girlfriend,' she laughed, 'or the first few dates at least. You remember what they're like? Having dinner, holding hands, a bit of emotional connection.'

'With sex?'

'Well, it's pretty unusual for clients not to want sex, or to at least not to think they do. Although it does happen of course.'

'Ok. So what about OWO?' I sounded out the vowels. Whatever they stood for, it sounded faintly depressing.

'Simple. Oral without.'

'Without what?'

'Tony, c'mon. Take a wild guess. Oral without a condom. A blow job.' I'd certainly never see that little acronym in the same way again. 'And CIM?'

'Ok we're getting a bit explicit now,' Amanda warned. 'Don't be shocked Tony. Cum in mouth.'

'Ok, got it, thanks,' I said, feeling my cheeks burning even in the empty flat. 'And swiftly moving on, what does A levels mean?' There was a brief pause on the other end of the line.

'Ok, maybe it's time to use your imagination for this one, Tony', she giggled. 'What do you think the A might stand for?' The only word that came into my head was 'Amanda'.

'Amanda, I have no idea,' I said. But I'm guessing it has nothing to do with Giselle's education.'

'Ok Tony, to be blunt again, because I don't have much time now, we're talking anal sex.' If you were looking for a sugar coating, Amanda definitely wasn't the person to provide it for you.

THE AGENCY

*

I'd sent Barry the profiles of the first group of girls I was planning to work with, and he'd got straight back to me the next day with an update on his progress. He was ready to start uploading photos and biographies to the site, and invited me back down to Southend so I could learn how to do that for myself, and he talk me through all his emailed instructions I'd so spectacularly failed to take in. When I thought back to myself at school, struggling to get to grips with IT, I couldn't help thinking all I'd really have needed to be a grade A student was Barry and his specialist curriculum.

It was only a month since I'd been down on the coast meeting him for the first time, but we were already into another season now. As we drove along the seafront, the sky was grey, and the beaches, that had been thronged with sun worshippers only a few short weeks ago, were deserted but for a few layered-up dog walkers bending into a bracing sea breeze.

We sat in the kitschy glamour of his office, the golden Britt Ekland at one end and meteor bursts of tropical fish at the other, and he talked me through the uploading process, every so often intoning 'what a stunner,' as his fingers played the keyboard like a virtuoso, and a photo of one of the girls flashed up on a monitor.

'So did you ever throw the balls up that Amanda sort?' he asked, as he brought up her images and started demonstrating how to resize them.

'Well actually Barry...'

'You fucking lucky sod!' he cut in, before I'd had the chance to even confirm or deny.

'But you can't afford to blow that kind of money.'

'Free of charge,' I couldn't help boasting.

'You jammy bastard!' he beamed. 'Was she good?'

'She was amazing, her body's unbelievable,' I admitted, feeling proud and a little shoddy for talking about it.

'You don't need to tell me mate, I can see it,' he said. 'It's one of those perks of the job son, good luck to you.' It didn't seem the time to tell him I couldn't stop thinking about her.

'Your girls are stunning,' he said, 'and by the looks of things', now uploading a shot of Vanessa, naked as the day she was born and floating in the frothy Jacuzzi of some five star hotel bathroom, 'a bit on the naughty side too.'

He let me take over uploading the last few profiles then, when we were done, started talking me through the advertising packages he was setting up for me.

'These are the main players you'll want to advertise with, bearing in mind your

budget,' he said, clicking between a series of sites. 'They're all good guys. I'll set up the initial ads with you, and over the weeks you'll learn how to maintain them. Nothing too complicated. These are standard directories where all the decent London agencies advertise, with links back to your website, and then there are a few review sites where clients read up on the girls. Sounds a bit seedy, but you can't beat word of mouth. I'm doing you some small banners, and some featured listings showing your top girls like that Amanda sort, you lucky sod,' he added, swapping to another monitor to show me these. 'The bigger ones are a couple of hundred quid a month, some of the smaller sites a couple of hundred a year, but it only takes one client to come from that and you've made your money back.'

I really needed to ask Barry how much a month's advertising was going to set me back and, while I asked him, to sound as relaxed about it as I could. Once I'd settled his web design fee, I reckoned I'd have about two grand to cover the advertising, and to keep the business and myself afloat until it started making money.

'At the moment your maximum monthly spend is only going to be two grand,' he said, swatting the figure away as though he was talking about twenty quid. 'To be honest with you Chris, that's your bare minimum, it's not worth setting up a campaign for less than that. Consider Rob's gonna be spending ten times what you are. But I know it's early days for you, and two grand will definitely get the ball rolling.'

Wiped out! That was all my savings pretty much taken care of, and no guarantee this thing was even going to work. I'm sure Barry could sense my apprehension, probably see the colour slowly draining from my cheeks, as I took it on the chin and thanked him for all he'd done.

'You know when Hugh Heffner started Playboy,' he said after an uncomfortable little silence, 'he started with nothing, right? Just the money for a mail-out to a few thousand blokes asking them to subscribe to a magazine that didn't even exist. Used the money they sent him to put together the first issue. A few years from now Chris, and you could well be the proud owner of your own little playmates' grotto.'

I think he could sense his story hadn't completely worked its intended magic.

'Why don't we give Rob a call,' he said, 'let him know how well our boy's getting on.'

# 7: We have lift-off

It was time to start meeting the girls, and this presented a bit of a dilemma. Inviting them to the man cave was out of the question; it was either going to terrify or depress them. These were Zone One girls after all, I doubted they had even heard of Wembley and my flat, even at its best, wasn't exactly a shining advertisement for the area.

I tried to imagine one of these stunning women, fresh from some Mayfair penthouse, perched on the edge of my lumpy old sofa and politely brushing away cat hairs as she calculated how soon she could make her excuses and run. But Rob had impressed on me how important it was to meet the women I was going to be working with, to get a feel for how they held themselves, how they spoke, whether they were friendly and reliable. In short, if they'd be a good fit for an elite agency.

It was Amanda who came up with the solution, a neutral location somewhere central and discreet where we could have an unhurried chat and get a feel for how we'd work together. I knew exactly the spot, a stylish little Italian café on the King's Road, all tucked-away little booths, that was buzzing with city types in the mornings and evenings but empty in the afternoons, besides a few eccentric old ladies dressed up in Vivienne Westwood, and homesick Polish nannies meeting other homesick Polish nannies.

The King's Road was renowned for its trendy bars and restaurants, and the sorts of expensive little boutiques that competed to attach the most outlandish price tag to a hand-knitted sweater. While I was waiting for the girls at the café, I'd watch the beautiful people who bought these things walking down from Sloane Square, tanned and glowing even in the late October chill, as the first leaves settled on pavements and the gusts that had blown them there twisted at oversized store bags.

This part of London wasn't exactly intimidating, but it wasn't inclusive either. If these girls could appear at home here, to be blunt amongst the wives of their potential clients, I could be fairly sure they were up to the job. It was a strange process entering a culture that you weren't born into, as I already knew from my Harrods days. You started out by faking it, adopting the entitled mannerisms, losing that over-eagerness to please. There was nothing inherently clever about it, it was just another way of behaving, a different code, and after a while it fitted like a second skin.

These girls would all be doing the same, some by instinct, others by observation. They had the added challenge of the language barrier of course but the best, like Amanda, could even turn that to their advantage, holding on to their seductive Latina accents not by accident but by design.

In the last week of October I almost lived in that little café on The King's Road, jittery on cappuccinos and macchiatos, and a constant stream of unfolding beauty. Giselle was the first of the girls to meet me there, a bit of a dress run to get my confidence up. I watched her sidle into the café in a three quarter length Burberry coat, belted tight at the waist, that I knew from Harrods would have set her back at least a couple of grand. The effect was faultless high-class call girl: an hourglass silhouette, and under it, she could have been naked but for her stilettoes and moulded Gucci sunglasses.

As we leaned in to kiss, I took in her heart-shaped face, the model's high cheekbones, and those full, pouty lips. 'Antonio, you did it. I'm so excited for you!' she congratulated, unbuttoning her coat and disabusing me of the fantasy that was all there would be against her skin. 'Do you like the photos I sent?' she asked, as I caught the waiter's eye and ordered a couple of coffees. 'Sorry they have to be blurred, I can't show my face because of my modelling. And my work name is Clarissa, by the way.'

'Ok, from now on let's just use that, to avoid any confusion,' I told her, noting it down in another little black book and wondering how I was going to keep up with all these aliases, as she carefully folded and smoothed the Burberry mac.

'I don't have long I'm afraid,' she continued, 'but I do need to talk to you briefly about clients. I'm not comfortable seeing young guys, they ask too many questions. I prefer to meet middle-aged men. No one over sixty though.' So far, it had been a master class in time management, a seamless sixty second transition from supportive friend to no-nonsense business partner. 'I'm sure you'll make a lot of middle aged men very happy,' I joked, feeling the thrilling pressure of her hand now over mine. 'And I only meet one on one, or duo with another girl,' she continued, blanking my attempt at humour and sliding away her hand as the waiter placed our coffees in front of us. 'You can book me with Amanda, she probably told you we do a great lesbian show.' There was just the flicker now of a mischievous smile. 'As for services, I love having sex, and I especially love A levels and CIM. Do you understand Antonio?' I nodded to show that I did, feeling I should be asking her to lower her voice, but not wanting to interrupt her confident flow. 'My rates,' she smiled knowingly, only now pausing to take a first sip of her espresso, 'four hundred first hour, additional hour three hundred, eighteen hundred overnight. Dinner dates and international bookings negotiable depending on where you send me and for how long.'

Clarissa, as I needed to start thinking of her, had talked

me through all I needed to know about her as a client in less than fifteen minutes, and that was the pattern of the meetings that followed, as the girls instructed me in what they wanted to do and how they wanted to do it. From the outset I'd decided to be honest with them about my inexperience; there was no point trying to bluff a knowledge of an industry they knew a lot better than me, after all. Just because I wasn't going to be caught out didn't mean I wasn't as nervous as hell though, sitting across from the sorts of stunning, ballsy women who had every right to be dismissive of my agent's credentials.

Over the week that followed, a stunning girl would generally walk into the café, and look straight past me as I sat there smiling at her in my designer suit. When I'd managed to attract her attention and assure her I was the person she'd come to meet, I'd invite her over to my tucked away little booth, and thank her for coming and giving me a chance, when I understood she was used to working for more established agencies. She'd soon be telling me I looked too young to be starting an agency, that Amanda had said I was a lovely guy who was going to be the next big thing, but hadn't mentioned my cute little baby face. I began to see how being around the same age as these girls actually had its advantages. We went to the same places, listened to the same kinds of music, and were pretty much all starting out on the same journey. All of these things, as well as my 'cute little baby face', worked to break the ice, and helped us cover a lot of ground very quickly.

For the main part Amanda had done a great job of pre-screening: the girls were already with top agencies, set up in luxury apartments all over central London, and all had professional portfolios. We discussed the days and times they wanted to work, who they wanted to see and who they were happy to work with. Some were happy seeing couples, and I was surprised at how many were bi-curious and keen to work with another girl on joint bookings.

Some told me they weren't comfortable seeing black or Arab guys. At first I was a little offended on behalf of the black friends I'd grown up with, even if they'd probably never see an escort anyway, and surprised girls from such diverse backgrounds would be so intolerant. They were at pains to explain though it wasn't about race, but about size: length with black guys and girth with Arabs, and I had to respect their wishes, even if it was going to complicate things at my end.

I was constantly amazed at just how open-minded these girls were, some just plain kinky. Angelina, a sweet Brazilian blonde based in Marylebone, with a 'butter wouldn't melt' demeanour, couldn't stop talking about how much she loved deep throating. A Venezuelan beauty queen and wannabe actress called Gabriella with a pied-a-terre in Notting Hill said she got a kick from being filmed, loved all the role playing and hiding behind masks. She described parties she'd been to that sounded like something out of Kubrick's *Eyes Wide Shut*. Another Brazilian stunner, Rebecca, who had an apartment hidden behind Selfridges, offered rimming as one of her specialities, which I had to get her to explain meant licking a client's bum. Never in my life would I have expected to find myself in a coffee shop on the King's Road, a stream of stunning women sharing how comfortable they were with double pen and clients shooting over them. I hoped any eavesdroppers would just assume we were talking about football.

The devil was in the detail, and every girl's availability had to be gone into. Denise could only work in the UK because of visa issues. Angelina and Bella only took Central London bookings because of study and other work commitments, and because Bella had a boyfriend who didn't know she escorted. Christina on the other hand, a super-busty Colombian based in South Ken, was happy to fly out of London at a moment's notice, if it was made worth her while. She had already been paid a mouth-watering sum to spend a month in Dubai as the guest of a wealthy Arab, and had several expat regulars there who rewarded her with serious oil money.

Some girls invited me directly to their apartments to discuss terms, and these were the ones I met last, in their Belgravia Mews houses, their ultra-modern Canary Wharf apartments and their Chelsea hideaways. I realised too late how valuable these visits were. They offered insights into the level of hospitality they could offer, and I got to understand access, and learn about nearby landmarks I could reference with clients when I was providing directions.

It also allowed for chance encounters with flatmates. Escorts, unsurprisingly, lived with other escorts, and the Brazilian girls in particular were always cooking and inviting me for lunches, which were fun in themselves but also a great recruitment opportunity. The girls loved to make fun of me, sitting at the dining table, a fork in one hand and a biro in the other, as I took down the details of potential new recruits. They'd say I was more like a journalist getting a story than an agency owner.

The more girls I visited, the more I started to see London for what it truly was: one gigantic red light district that stretched from Canary Wharf in the east all the way over to Chelsea in the west. I'd naively assumed London's real sex industry was confined to Soho, but that was one of the few areas of central London this new breed of high-end international call girl seemed to avoid: they said it was too tacky, too noisy, too dirty, lacked exclusivity. As Rob would say, you live and learn.

*

And then in November 2005 the site went live. November the ninth, to be exact, easy to verify because it was the day the European Space Agency launched its Venus space shuttle. Despite the desolate launch footage from some barren former Soviet Republic, it seemed auspicious, and wickedly appropriate, a cosmic mission to the planet of love on the day I hoped to be launching my own rockets left, right and centre. Some expert had said the mission wouldn't reach Venus for an estimated six months but, with the precarious state of my finances, my mission needed to be bearing fruit a lot sooner.

Barry had phoned me the night before the launch to let me know the site was ready, and all the girls' profiles had been uploaded (there were fifteen in total now), and Amanda had made sure everyone available that Wednesday had been primed to expect calls. We were ready to go live: a midweek start should be quieter, what we called in retail a 'soft opening' so any glitches could be ironed out without undue pressure.

I'd talked to Amanda and she'd said all the girls were really excited. There was such a good vibe I was beginning to think we should have had some sort of launch party. I had such a great team around me, I felt buoyed up on all the good will, a reborn Tony, the figurehead and fulcrum of a shedload of dreams. There was nothing left to do now but sit back and wait for the calls.

And so ten a.m. came and I waited. I had my two phones

lined up side by side on the coffee table next to the sofa, a black Nokia for the agency line and a silver Nokia to contact the girls. Nothing in the first five minutes, and there was actually a palpable relief. I had time to settle down and relax. The first hour passed. I watched the first replay of the rocket launch on News 24, a red strip of recap summary spooling along the bottom of the screen. Half an hour later it replayed again.

By midday I must have watched the Venus launch four or five times over, and was getting impatient. The business line finally rang soon after, but it was just Barry checking up on me. 'How's it going mate?' he asked tentatively.
'Quiet mate. Nothing yet. Plenty of messages from the girls though, keeping me informed and up to date.' I probably sounded a bit deflated. 'Don't worry mate, hang in there,' he said, 'I know it's gonna work for you, give it time.'

I sorted a Pot Noodle for my lunch, thinking that at this rate I'd be living on a lot of Pot Noodles. The kettle was only three steps from my sofa, but I took the black phone with me just to be sure I didn't miss a call, and let the noodles cool before I started in on them, small mouthfuls so I wouldn't get caught with my pants down. Nothing. I took solace in my notepads for a while, refreshing my knowledge of the girls and being shocked all over again at their prices, as I sat learning their locations and stats by heart, height, hair colour, body type, anything to fill the time.

I'd had my fill of News 24 by the early afternoon, every successful lift-off with its whoops and shrieks from mission control a censure of my own agency's refusal to launch. Sticking with the space theme, I reached for my Bond collection and slid *Moonraker* into the VCR, hoping a bit of Roger Moore would calm the nerves.

Around four o'clock, it was Amanda's turn to check up on me. Along with all the other girls, she'd been sending me texts throughout the day, letting me know she was still available. She'd guessed I suppose things weren't going so well.

'Hey Tony, Mr. Soprano, what's up?'

'Still waiting,' I answered, trying to hold everything together. All the good fortune I'd had in finding Rob, Barry and Amanda, each with their own charmed lives, and now all that luck seemed to have just vanished. I'd thrown away a steady job most people would have killed for, sunk my life savings, such as they were, into this odd little dream, and maybe that was all it was going to prove to be. And if that was the case I'd be out on the street in twenty-one days and counting; this month's rent had left the cupboard bare. I could feel the mounting stress as she reassured me things would get busier, not to worry, and signed off blowing kisses down the phone.

At seven o'clock, a full nine hours after I'd opened for

business, the agency phone started ringing. I was busy making myself some cheese on toast, and I remember turning and looking back in shock at the business line skittering across my coffee table, and even hesitating for a second, maybe two, before I answered. Whatever was about to unfold on the other end of that line, some unsuspecting guy was about to launch the agency, and my new life along with it.

My first ever client was asking, in an accent I was working hard to place (Eastern European possibly?) if Clarissa was available. His tone of voice was so polite and respectful, and the process itself so straightforward, none of the nightmare scenarios I'd been imagining all day - heavy breathing weirdos, time wasters, guys haggling over prices - that it seemed almost too easy.

'No problem at all sir,' I heard myself saying. 'Just allow me a moment to contact the young lady, and I'll get straight back to you to confirm.' I put down the agency phone and picked up the second line.

'Hey Antonio?' Clarissa answered.

'Hi hun, I have a booking for you. Two hour in-call.'

'Wonderful, what time?'

'Eight o'clock. Seven hundred?'

'Perfect.'

'Ok, give me a minute and I'll text back to confirm.'

If I was bag-of-nerves excited, Clarissa couldn't have sounded more laid back. I could almost hear her impatience to get off the line to strip and shower. I called the client back. 'Hello sir, sorry for keeping you waiting,' I heard myself apologising, even if I knew it had been less than two minutes since our first call. 'Clarissa has confirmed eight p.m. sir. I'll send you her location now. Can I please take your name to pass on to her? Thank you Mr. Dmitri, and please call me if you have any problems.'

Text book customer service, even if I said so myself. I'd taken Harrods to the very heart of my business from my very first call, and handled it just the way Rob had advised: 'turn the calls round quick, after all time's money, young fella.' There was a stab of pride that took me by surprise, as I imagined Mr. Dmitri probably picturing me in some swanky office somewhere, rushed off my feet connecting the beautiful and the well connected. I texted Clarissa to confirm, then sent my first text to my first client detailing the fee and address. Then there was nothing to do but sit back and wait.

And the thing about waiting is you have time to discover all the doubts that haven't until now had any solid foundation to build around. My first booking. Had Clarissa fully understood the time and details? Was Mr. Dmitri as decent as he seemed? Was he even Mr. Dmitri? I wondered if clients gave fake names too, I supposed they did. Could it really be this straightforward? There must be something I hadn't thought of. I was finally sharing the nervy excitement of mission control.

At 8.02 she sent a text confirming he was with her. We had lift off. She signed off with a flurry of kisses, like tiny stars in a night sky.

And so that was how it happened: my first booking for my first high class escort, when just a few months before I hadn't even known what the word meant, or that this world even existed. And now that Mr. Dmitri had made it to the apartment, what could possibly go wrong?

Inevitably, I started thinking about *everything* that could go wrong, not helped by a spate of distant sirens: a psychotic client, a guy who wouldn't pay, a kitchen knife, a crime scene. I forced myself to calm down. Clarissa knew what she was doing after all, and Amanda would hopefully be around too, if for some reason things did get messy.

As time passed, my mind started wandering in other directions, wondering what Clarissa and her Mr. Dmitri were getting up to, picturing them as a hot movie couple, Richard Gere and Julia Roberts in *Pretty Woman*, Marlon Brando and Maria Schneider in *Last Tango in Paris*. An older guy, a beautiful woman, sparks flying, sexual combustion. At 10,05 the all clear came through from Giselle, 'Thanks hun, he's just left kiss kiss'. We'd done it! She had just earned a pile of money, and so had I, the easiest money I'd ever made.

I was still coming down from the drama, and congratulating myself on a successful first booking, when the business line rang again. This time it was a well-spoken English guy, wanting to know who was available at short notice. He was at Victoria Station, probably delaying heading home to his wife and kids, and I automatically thought of Tamara, close by in Belgravia. 'Tell me about her,' he asked, apparently now with all the time in the world. 'Sir, you'll find her details and her portfolio on our website,' I answered, keeping it short and sweet. There was the same phone juggling routine as before, leaving me amazed once again at how efficiently Rob's system worked. Tamara was still free, she could be ready to meet in thirty minutes, a quick 'x' to confirm his arrival, and, just over an hour later, another to let me know he'd left and all was well.

I stayed up until two a.m. on the sort of high I imagined you got as an actor stepping off stage, and needing to chill out and come down from the buzz. A few more texts came in from girls letting me know they were free or fully booked for the night, and it wasn't until I was getting ready for bed that I noticed I must have been smoking like a trooper all day: there was a toxic smog of fumes hovering over the flat, and cigarette butts filled every ashtray I owned.

Feeling like a conscientious shopkeeper, I mentally tallied up the day's takings, and realised I'd just earned more money than I ever had in a single day in my life. I couldn't help phoning Amanda. She knew about Clarissa's booking, and she was just as pleased for Tamara, and for me, when I told her how much I'd made.

'And you're going to make a lot more,' she said. And when Amanda said something, I'd learned to believe it.

I crashed into bed thinking about where this newly minted career could take me, and dreaming of chauffeur-driven Mercs and a business that was a licence to print money. It wouldn't be long before things started to get a bit more complicated, but ignorance is bliss, and I was already looking forward to ten a.m. when I'd be fresh and rested and manning my phones all over again, and they would no doubt be ringing off the hook.

# 8: The Latin connection

Out of blue the next morning Rob called to check up on me. I'd got up feeling distinctly un-fresh and unrested, the two packs of Marlborough Lights probably playing their part, and the flat was so cold and toxic-smelling that Bubbles, normally clawing for her breakfast, was nowhere to be seen. An early client call, from another English guy, had felt more like work than the day before, and when Emelia texted to let me know the client had been a no-show (a single question mark), I was in no mood to be messed about. I'd called him a couple of times, no response, and sent a follow-up text asking him to get back to me, but again nothing. I'd phoned Emelia after that to commiserate, thinking of all the trouble she'd have gone to, and all the time she'd have wasted. 'Hun I'm so sorry, he's not answering,' I'd told her, feeling the need to apologise on behalf of this dickhead.

'Tony, don't worry, it's not your fault, this happens, you're always going to get these idiots,' she'd placated, turning the tables on me. 'It's just part of the business, you'll get used to it.'

That call with Emelia had underscored how lucky I was to have this great group of girls working with me, and that was exactly what I'd said to Rob.

'These girls are really on the ball,' I'd told him when I could get a word in edgeways, 'they tell me when they're up in the morning, they tell me when they're off to the gym, they're so organised they put me to shame.'

'Well mate, you are working with a particular quality of girl,' he'd reminded me, though I could tell from his tone he was quietly impressed too. When I mentioned the no-show, it was his turn to commiserate. 'Ah scumbag,' he'd pronounced, 'but I'm afraid you will get these time wasters, don't let it get you down.'

'But I don't understand, why would someone make a booking and then not turn up?'

'It happens,' he said, 'maybe something came up, maybe his plans changed. But listen mate, get used to it, it's part of the business.' And after a calculated pause, 'Look Tony, I've dug up some useful numbers for you, some of the top photographers linked to the business, and letting agents who specialise in finding flats for working girls. These will be useful for when you get new girls on your books. '

I was a bona fide agency owner now, with more than a dozen girls already relying on me to get them work, and plans to take on a lot more, but these were all contingencies that hadn't even crossed my mind. 'Rob, I can't thank you enough for everything you've done to help me out,' I'd told him, 'I really owe you one.'

'We've gotta look after the new young fella on the block,' he'd joked, making light of it all.

I told him how exciting my first day had been, but how stressed I'd felt waiting for the phone to ring, setting up the bookings, and waiting for confirmation from the girls that everything was going to plan. 'My nerves have been jangling a bit,' I confided, 'and to be honest Rob I feel a bit shot this morning. I had a bit of a sleepless night turning it all over in my head.'

'There's no turning back, you're in it now fella,' he replied. I couldn't decide at the time if his words sounded ominous or reassuring. 'But come on mate,' he'd chivvied me along, 'no risk no reward.'

He was keen to know how I'd handled the first couple of clients, and I talked him through what I'd done and said, hoping to impress him with how quick my turnaround had been. It was reassuring to hear him say I was hitting all the right notes, asking for and giving out all the key information the clients and the girls needed. We must have spent a good ten minutes going through it all. It felt like a military debrief.

'You're an absolute natural Tony,' Rob concluded at the end of it, 'are you sure you've never done this before? And by the way mate, I've had a look at your site, it's class, really looks the business. Barry's done a brilliant job. And what a selection of girls, all absolute stunners! You pretty much have the whole of South America covered, you truly have the Latin connection.'

I told him about the meetings I'd had with the girls at the café on the King's Road, recounting how embarrassing it had been discussing sexual services among all those Chelsea housewives. 'I'm still in shock at how naughty a lot of the girls are to be honest Rob, I can't believe girls this hot would do so much kinky shit,' I told him.

'Get used to it mate,' he laughed, 'these girls don't fuck about, and London's full of birds like this. It's early days, but you've got off to a good start Tony, and let me tell you, it only gets better from this point on. Barry's set you up with a half decent ad campaign, considering the money you've put in. Give it time, and you'll get some great regulars, and they'll be the driving force of the business. And once you've got the trust of some of your more exclusive clients, that's when you and your girls will find yourselves invited to some very special events. You'll get to see a side of London you never knew existed.'

'What do you mean?' I asked him, 'parties?'

'I'm talking gang bangs, swingers' parties, Mayfair mansions, exclusive gentlemen's clubs. Invitation only, all very hush-hush. I promise you Tony, when you see what goes on at these things, and who's involved, your eyes will be popping out of your head.' It was a promise that made me think of Gabriella, and the *Eyes Wide Shut* parties she'd described in the café on the King's Road. Everything I'd seen and done so far, all the events and conversations that had already blown my mind, were all just an entrée, it seemed, to the main, mind-blowing event.

*

Later that morning, I had a call from Amanda inviting me over to hers for lunch, a great opportunity to see her again, and to collect my first commission from Clarissa while I was about it. I dressed to impress in a sharp designer suit, and headed out into the sudden winter chill of Wembley High Road, jumping on the same number bus I used to take to work. It may have been an old routine, but it came with a new levity, no longer the prelude to an eight hour shift stuck behind my Harrods counter.

Looking out from the bus window at the same old London going about its business, delivery drivers in their white vans, construction workers in their hard hats, it would have been easy to believe nothing had changed. Your life turned upside down, and from the outside no one noticed a thing. I guessed that was how everyone, Rob, Amanda, the hedge fund managers, the oligarchs, got away with it. No one cared all that much, no one was even really watching.

For old times' sake, I jumped out close to Harrods and wandered down to Amanda's from there. The Harrods windows, as I sauntered past, had a between-seasons feel, the tired autumn displays already down and the visual merchandisers getting ready to work their magic on the Christmas ones. Thank God I'd be missing that rollercoaster ride, even if it felt strange all of a sudden not to be a part of it.

As was our habit now, when I got to Amanda's, the apartment door was open onto the hallway, and I could see the girls inside already cooking. Clarissa was lifting a spoonful a sauce to her lips from a pot on the hob, and pulling a face, and Amanda was reacting by adding what I guessed was salt. They both looked stunning, casually gorgeous in skimpy vests and shorts, so I wasn't sure whether they had even dressed, or were still in their night things.

Strange that I never thought of the two of them alone here together, sharing all those domestic moments flatmates shared, cooking, and gossiping in that impenetrable Portuguese they switched from as soon as they saw me. I advanced on the island, and they surrounded me in a pincer movement, loading me with kisses and hugs so there was nothing for it but to submit. Clarissa dipped her finger into a smaller pot of the cooling sauce and lifted it to my mouth.

'You like?' she said.

'I like,' I replied, absolutely no idea what I was tasting.

Lunch was feijoada, one of Clarissa's favourite dishes, a thick brown stew sticky with beans and pork, and Amanda had cracked open a couple of bottles of red, to celebrate the launch of the agency she said, and Clarissa's first job with me. I knew these girls would use any event as an excuse for wine, and there was no point refusing, even if I was officially supposed to be working.

The lunch was interrupted every so often by text messages from the other girls, and Clarissa took each opportunity to scroll through my phone, checking up on their whereabouts as they signed on and off. Over coffee she disappeared to her room and came back with a stuffed envelope. 'Your Mr. Dmitri was the perfect client Antonio,' she said, 'not too young, not too old, very sweet. We talked for most of the booking. Two hours, and he only fucked me once. It was easy.'

'That's great,' was all I managed to get out in reply. Taking the envelope and stuffing it into my breast pocket, I noticed Amanda's lips curling around her espresso cup. Clarissa meanwhile leaned over to give me a little peck on the cheek, then headed back to her room, leaving Amanda and me to move out onto the balcony with what was left of the second bottle of wine. 'You'll get used to her,' Amanda said, 'it's just work, we talk about it like you would about customers at Harrods. By the way, always count the money in front of the girl.'

Since we'd had sex a month ago now, right here in this apartment, so much had happened. I'd thought a lot about that day, but my thoughts never seemed to take me anywhere. With Amanda none of the normal rules applied, there were no obvious next steps. Take this afternoon. Right now, the two of us finally alone, she seemed more curious to know what I thought of Clarissa. Did I think she was hot? Who did I prefer of the two of them? There was no hint of jealousy in her questioning, just a weighted curiosity, and the sense of a mind mischievously at work on some larger plan.

Her interrogation was interrupted by the skittering of my business phone across the balcony table. It was an American guy, staying at the Dorchester, and enquiring in his deep southern drawl if I had any busty girls free to join him there that afternoon. This would be my first outcall. I looked across the table at Amanda, mouthed 'outcall ASAP?' and she nodded eagerly back. This wasn't exactly the way I'd imagined us spending our afternoon together.

I directed the American to her online profile, and he couldn't agree terms fast enough, I guess unable to believe his luck. Taking his name and room number so I could phone him back at the hotel to confirm (another of Rob's little tricks), we agreed Amanda would meet him there in an hour, and she disappeared into her room to change while I paced the balcony, working through a few more cigarettes, and trying to make sense of what had just happened.

When Amanda emerged from her bedroom, she looked stunning in a little black cocktail dress that wrapped around her curves and showcased her stunning boobs, a silver Tiffany pendant quaking between them as she stepped across the room in her Jimmy Choos.

We hailed a taxi from right outside her apartment block. It was one of those lulls between gridlock, and as the cab glided through the grey streets, and we sat silently side by side, I took stock of what was happening. I was speeding across Central London with a Brazilian beauty about to hire her body to a wealthy American at one of London's top luxury hotels. A scenario probably being played out invisibly all over the city, and made possible by global economics and guys like me.

I caught our cabbie, old school in a shirt and tie, scrutinising the pair of us in his rear-view mirror. Did he have any idea what we were up to? A good looking twenty-something couple dressed to the nines, and hailing a cab from their South Ken apartment to one of London's swankiest hotels? Or was he as blind as everyone else to this secret London? I turned to face Amanda. 'Do outcalls ever get difficult?' I asked her, in something like a whisper.

'Not really,' she said, it wasn't in the interests of the hotels to make a fuss, even if it was pretty obvious what was going on, a stunning woman turning up unaccompanied in the early afternoon, and leaving a couple of hours later. The hotel staff was there to ensure their clients had everything they wanted after all; there were concierges who went out of their way to build their own industry connections. I wondered if that explained Rob's royal reception at the Royal Garden Hotel.

When the cab pulled up outside The Dorchester, Amanda turned to kiss me on the cheek and, stepping out of the cab, said she'd text me to let me to know everything was fine. I watched her killer figure disappear into the dark interior of the hotel's lobby, the door held obligingly open by a top-hatted doorman. 'Lovely looking girl, if you don't mind me saying mate,' the cabbie commented as I handed him a twenty from Clarissa's envelope. 'You want to hold on to that one.'

'Ah no, we're just friends,' I admitted, telling him to keep the change.

I crossed Park Lane and wandered into Hyde Park, finding myself unexpectedly in Speakers' Corner. A few old men were standing on boxes, speaking in projected voices about the Iraq War, freedom of speech, socialism, no one really listening but a few tourists taking photos anyway. A call came through on the business line and I arranged a booking, this time for Lola based over on the Fulham Road, then wandered around a little aimlessly, imagining the scene I'd just set up between Amanda and her loaded American, all the while the words of the cabbie playing through my mind.

# 9: No more secrets

Late November was finding its groove of cold, misty mornings and dark, frosty evenings and I was starting to feel out the rhythm of the agency, its lusty currents and twisty little vortexes.

After the chaotic head-rush of the first few days, a shaky pattern was starting to emerge as the weeks pushed forward: a slow trickle of bookings through late morning into early afternoon that surged from six until midnight, and cascaded hard into the weekends. There were some low-key days when, for whatever reason, the evening rush just never came, but it was all about learning to marshal your time and use those quiet hours to update profiles, tweak ads and rotate the girls' featured profiles on the site.

The Christmas season was within touching distance now, and I could smell its promise in the frosty air. When Rob called, we'd still swap war stories and engage in some great banter, but he'd always finish up by making the serious point that however many bookings I was getting right now, in the weeks building up to the party season I'd be getting a lot busier.

I couldn't wait. I had a naughty Advent calendar Amanda had cheekily handed me along with her last commission, and I'd be opening window number one in just a couple of days now. The calendar itself was an outrageous sacrilege, a holy boob-fest, but these South American girls managed to synthesise religion and sex and somehow square the circle.

I'm sure most people, making their own assumptions about my new line of work, would have been shocked to discover just how routine my working day actually was. After falling exhausted into bed around two, I'd still be up early, scrolling through my texts from the girls to get a picture of how their days were looking. I'd fry up some bacon and eggs over my morning quota of two cigarettes (I was trying to cut down now my stress levels were more under control), rattle some dried food into Bubbles' dish, eat my greasy English, then be on it and manning the phones by ten o'clock. I'd switch on my TV and ease myself into the day soon after, flicking from chat shows to property programmes and back again while I waited for my first call.

Afternoons, I'd gotten into the habit of reaching for a box set and sticking on some favourite Sopranos action, reliving my namesake Tony Soprano's adventures as he reluctantly headed into therapy for his panic attacks (a taste of things to come), argued with his wife, shagged a stunning pole dancer or dispatched a troubling rival to sleep with the fishes. All the while taking more bookings, tweaking the site and strategizing how I was going to keep the agency moving forwards.

I watched this show differently since I'd set up the agency, and now felt an odd kinship with Mr. Soprano. Tony and I were both living two lives, after all. He was a New Jersey family man who just happened to also be a mob boss; I was a working class Wembley boy who just happened to also run an agency of stunning elite escorts. Reality could be just as strange as fiction, it turned out. Almost every day now I was arranging bookings at some of most iconic hotels in London, Claridge's, The Savoy and The Ritz. When I was working at Harrods I was used to interacting with these hotels, arranging for couriered shopping to be delivered, but now I was arranging for a very different kind of personal delivery. The really odd thing was how seamlessly it had begun to feel like a regular kind of life. Do something over and over and it's surprising how quickly the bizarre becomes a habit.

\*

As I got to grips with the stresses and strains of my new life, I saw how seriously I'd been neglecting my old one, and I was annoyed at myself for letting my oldest friends fall off the radar. In the twelve odd years since we'd all left school, we'd stuck together pretty much through thick and thin, glued by a shared love of football, our on-off relationship dramas, and probably the fact none of us had been adventurous enough to start new lives elsewhere.

But all that time, and all of that shared history, had to mean something. We'd witnessed each others' successes and failures, and had always tried to be there for each other as we took turns to find girlfriends, get dumped, move into our own places and get on with our own lives.

More importantly, we'd celebrated and commiserated together as, season after season, our footie teams walked the fine line of victory and defeat. We may have supported different clubs, but the rivalry was part of what brought us together. And now I'd hardly seen them since Chelsea, under The Special One, had won the premiership with a record ninety-five points, in another life it seemed now, way back before any of this madness had kicked in.

So I called Liam and Ryan, my two oldest friends, guys I'd known as far back as infant school, to rekindle a Saturday match day tradition, guessing at some point I'd have to catch them up on all my news.

I'd really missed hanging out with them, Liam part Irish, part Scottish and always excitable, Ryan the perfect counterpoint with his chilled Jamaican swagger. The prospect of meeting up set my mind racing over everything that had happened in the last few months, and how I was going to break it all to them. Right now, they didn't even know I'd left Harrods. But then how did you start that conversation? Tell two of your oldest mates you'd thrown in a ten year retail career to start an elite escort agency? I had absolutely no idea. I guessed it would all come out in the wash, one way or another, though fuck knows what they'd make of it all. I'd given up trying to second-guess other people's reactions, when even my own had taken me by surprise.

*

The guys arrived early for some pre-match banter, and I got the kettle on, even though typically the first thing Ryan had done was plonk down a bottle of brandy on the kitchen table.
'So what's this big news you were on about?' he cut to the chase, in his no nonsense, catch up where you left off kind of way.
'Well fellas,' I said, easing myself in, 'I've quit Harrods.'
'Why Chris?' it was Liam now who shot back, a shrill edge to his voice, 'I thought that was your dream job.'
'What's going on mate,' Ryan followed up, suddenly alert, looking round the flat and taking in the little changes, the scattered notepads and the two extra phones side by side on the

coffee table. 'You're not serving up are you?'

'Fuck Ryan!' I laughed out loud at the absurdity of the situation, 'No, I'm not dealing. It's a bit of a long story, but I met this Brazilian girl at work...' their eyes lighting up with a whole new level of interest... 'and she introduced me to this whole new world, this...'

'What the fuck are you on about?' Liam interrupted, irritated or impatient, I couldn't tell which, but pushing me to get to the point. This was it, no more secrets. 'Well this girl, her name's Amanda by the way, she's a high class escort, and she told me she really thought I had what it took to run an agency of my own, pushed me to give it a go. So that's why I've been off the radar for a while guys, my head's been buried in getting to grips with setting it all up.'

Either end of my sofa, like a couple of book ends, Liam and Ryan looked across at each other in a sort of shocked dumb show that lasted a couple of seconds at least, before they both cracked up in hysterics. It must have been a minute or longer before either of the guys could speak again. 'Stop fucking around, you're winding us up,' Ryan finally said, still giddy with the fun of it, enjoying the crack. 'Seriously guys, I'm not joking.' I was laughing myself now, despite my best efforts to stay composed and look serious. 'Ok look, I'll show you.'

I'd booted up the computer now the guys were

crouched either side of me, and their jaws were hanging as I navigated the site for them, proudly showing off all its features and clicking through the girls' stunning photos. They still weren't having any of it though, convinced it was all some elaborate hoax, April Fool's in early December.

This was raising all sorts of problems I hadn't even considered. How did you make someone believe something so out of the ordinary, so clearly improbable? I'd started to think of my agency life as normal, hadn't imagined that it would seem about as likely as dropping into conversation I was actually Father Christmas, or that I'd just been signed for Chelsea.

Scrambling for the solution, I clicked on the site's home page, pointed out the phone number displayed there and got Ryan to dial it, relishing his dumbfounded expression as the business phone started dancing little circles over my coffee table. Making the connection, the guys were shrieking all over again, in unison with it. 'Fuck Chris, so what you're a pimp now?' Liam challenged a bit breathily, once he'd had the chance to get over his initial shock.

'No I'm not,' I cut back, really not wanting them to get the wrong idea. 'I purely set up bookings, I'm just a glorified receptionist in theory. You can think of me as a middle man, but definitely not a pimp.'

I think neither of them could still quite believe it. I

could see the struggle on their faces to make sense of what they were being told as I patiently answered their questions about how Amanda had introduced me to the business, how I'd met all the girls now displayed half-naked in front of them, and how I'd set up the site they couldn't shift their eyes away from.

And even as they slowly processed the facts, I could see the jury was out. Liam was warily impressed, all 'look at you, Mr. Entrepreneur!' but Ryan was still stressing, maybe the joints he'd brought along weren't helping. He kept asking me if I really knew what I was getting myself into, had weighed up all the risks.

'You guys worry too much, you've watched far too much television,' I countered, topping up the brandies to help calm things down a bit.

We were still working our way through the site, and when we got to Amanda I pointed her out, so they could see for themselves how stunning she was. 'And believe it or not guys, I've actually shagged her,' I told them. I was getting a bit swimmy with the pot, and couldn't resist the boast. Maybe that swung it. I could see Liam slowly coming around now as he got more used to the idea, and started weighing up the potential perks of the job against its perceived dangers.

'You lucky bastard,' the guys almost chorused in stereo from either side of the computer.

'They're all absolutely beautiful mate,' Ryan added, but fuck they'd need to be for five hundred quid.' He'd clearly been looking at more than the photos. 'I know guys, don't get me started, it still shocks me every day, and five hundred is nothing, the average price,' I told him. 'Girls charge anything from four to eight hundred for a single hour.'

'What the hell do you get for that?' they laughed.

'Well, officially companionship. Between 'consenting adults' of course.' I air marked that classic phrase. 'But guys, these clients hand that sort of money over without batting an eye.'

Liam was now working his way through all the profiles, checking out the girls' locations. 'There are so many of them Chris, they're all over London, you've got them from Canary Wharf all the way over to Chelsea,' he said.

'The kind of guys who spend this kind of money are expecting to visit a top location, and quite frankly guys you're never going to find these kind of girls in Wembley,' I told him. For a split second we all looked out at the dull Wembley skyline in silent commiseration.

'And you're sure it's not dodgy?' Ryan took a toke on his joint, and passed it over to me, clearly now more relaxed, and willing to be reassured.

'Mate, I've been really lucky,' I said, doing my best to set his mind at rest. 'I've made some great contacts in the industry through this unbelievable web designer based out in Southend.

THE AGENCY

He's introduced me to another Essex boy who's one of the top guys. You wouldn't mess with either of them, I mean they're all Range Rovers, tats and Rolexes, but very successful at what they do and exactly the guys you want on your side.'

'OK Chris, but they still sound a bit like gangsters to me. Just promise me you'll be careful, alright?'

'Turn it in mate,' I said, touched by his concern even if I wasn't going to show it. 'They've definitely got a serious way about them, but I wouldn't call them gangsters.'

'Turn it in! What the fuck's that?' Ryan mocked. 'God, you're even starting to sound like them already.' Normal service was clearly being resumed.

'Maybe they have rubbed off on me a little guys,' I conceded. 'I went and spent the whole day with Barry down in Southend. He picked me up at the station, took me over to his hillside hideaway with these amazing views of the Essex coast, it reminded me of when we used to go down there on bank holidays. But obviously I was there for a very different reason.'

'You mean not to get pissed and pull birds?' Liam chimed in.

'We were too busy building this state of the art site, mate,' I bragged. 'And then Rob, the agency owner, met me for lunch at this unbelievable West End restaurant, gave me loads of great advice. Honestly, I wouldn't have been able to do any of it without them.'

'These guys sound proper serious Chris, are you sure you know what you've got yourself into?' Liam asked one last time.

'Honestly, don't worry Liam, it's cool. They've really taken me under their wing. They've even invited me to a West Ham game, they've got their own box at Upton Park. And they're both big into their boxing too, want me to go to a fight with them sometime. I will get around to it, but running the agency and manning these phones is the priority right now.'

'So it's working out for you?' Liam asked.

'Well it's early days guys, I've barely been open for a month, and I'm really having to put the hours in, but yeah, I've really hit the ground running,' I admitted. 'I've set up quite a few bookings already, there's really good money in this guys.'

During this little confessional Ryan had been busy navigating the site for himself, and had found Bella in Mayfair's profile, and his eyes were pretty much out on stalks.

'She is an absolute sort,' he emphasised every word, stressed every syllable. 'What are they like?' he asked, now a note of awe in his voice, like when he used to ask me about the celebs I'd served in Harrods.

'They're businesswomen mate, that 's the best way to put it,' I summarised, 'classy, sophisticated, professional, they're totally in control. *They* apply to the agency, *they* tell me when they want to work, *they* tell me what kinds of clients they're comfortable seeing and not seeing, and I purely work from *their* guidelines.'

'And what are the blokes like?'

'Well we call them clients, I told him. 'And the simplest way to put it is they're all fucking loaded.' They both chuckled. 'It's only a certain type of guy that would blow the best part of a couple of grand on a few hours with one of these birds.'

'Fuck me mate, you've gone from one of the best jobs ever in Harrods, to an even better one now,' Liam broke in. 'Is it even classed as a job?'

'It's fucking hard work mate,' I remonstrated, even if I was struggling to convince myself by this point.

'So hang on, just explain this to me one more time,' Ryan wanted to know, or maybe just to hear me tell the story again, 'this has all come about from running into some Brazilian tart on the roof of Harrods and she's talked you into setting up an agency? And you've just jumped ship, left Harrods and now you're fucking running one? Are you fucking winding us up?!'

'You've got it in one. That's pretty much exactly how it happened.' Put in those terms, it didn't stand up as the most convincing of stories. 'Guys there's more, she invited me to a wicked party at hers, everyone was off their faces, coke everywhere, and I got totally fucked on some really good pills with her and a couple of her mates....'

'How much better does this get?' Ryan interrupted. 'Money,

classy birds, coke-fuelled parties. And you've shagged one of them already!'

It was difficult not to seem smug, so I did my best to try and point out some of the negatives.

'I know it might sound easy sat here with my phones and the cat and you stone-heads having a laugh, but it can be quite draining actually,' I admitted. 'I do have a responsibility to make sure everything runs smoothly, and I do worry that the girls are safe. I've got a bit of a duty of care, even if there's only so much I can do stuck out here in Wembley, so it's a lot of pressure.'

'Oh, shut up, you lucky bastard,' Liam laughed, not having any of it. 'Who do you think you are, Hugh Heffner?'

'Talking of which, I'm way too stoned now mate,' I said. 'Don't let me smoke any more, ok? I really need to concentrate and stay focused for when the phone rings. You have no idea how much I have to remember. I've got to have the girls' locations and prices at my fingertips. Fuck, I've got notepads full of this stuff.' I took one from the coffee table and flicked through it to illustrate my point. 'And then I've got to try and suss out these clients, get a feel for who they are, if they're serious or just timewasters.'

The guys were just laughing now, a glazed disbelief settling over their faces. Just then, a text came through from one of the girls. 'Look, this is the typical kind of message I get,' I said, reading out a message from Vanessa, 'Hi honey, I'm off to the beauticians to have my eyebrows done,' she'd written, 'I'll be available in a couple of hours, I'll text you when I get home.' They found it hilarious, probably the weed talking. I took out a couple of my newly printed business cards, from the same printer that Amanda used, and handed them to the boys. 'Guys', I said, immediately having second thoughts, 'actually I'm not too sure I should give you one of these, I don't want them being found by your girlfriends when they drop out of your back pockets later on. Probably best not to tell them at all actually, or they'll never let you anywhere near me ever again.' They both smirked, and 'I can't wait to see what the rest of the lads are gonna say about this', Liam joked.

'Look mate,' I said, a little pulse of stress fighting the chill of the weed, 'please just leave that to me. I wasn't sure how you guys were going to react, what with your girlfriends and everything. I've got no idea how everyone else is going to take it.'

'Oh fuck 'em!' Ryan was hitting his stride now. 'Do your thing, and good luck to you,' he gave me his blessing, sounding remarkably like Rob as he did so.

The game had already finished, the result gone pretty much unnoticed, when the business line finally rang. The guys just stared at it, as though they'd never seen a ringing phone before. 'I've got to sober up and answer this,' I told them, putting a finger to my lips. They reacted with an awed silence, as I prepared to answer in my best Harrods voice.

It was a first booking for Sara over in Canary Wharf, the most expensive girl on the site, at eight hundred pounds for just one hour of her precious time, and as I worked my way through my script, I could sense the guys leaning into the phone, not wanting to miss a word. I grabbed the second line and texted Sara the offer of the booking, the guys dumbly looking on, as she responded instantly with an 'All confirmed, I can do that,' and I called the client back, running through what had by now become my practised spiel. I texted Sara back, waited for the delivery report, then put the phone down and looked across to Liam and Ryan.

They had been dead quiet for the whole three minutes it had taken to set up and confirm the booking, and even now sat staring at me and the phones, as if they were waiting for some next bizarre instalment. 'There you go guys,' I said, 'it's as simple as that. Unless I'm setting up an outcall, when it gets a bit more complicated.' They looked at me uncomprehendingly. 'But I'm way too stoned to explain that to you now,' I laughed. 'God, that was sorted in no time!' Liam said, visibly relaxing again. 'Are you serious that bloke is going to spend that kind of money?'

'Yep, if he turns up of course.'

For the rest of the evening Liam and Ryan were like a couple of kids in a sweet shop, albeit stoned and slightly tipsy kids, sitting there scrolling through half naked photos of stunning Brazilians, Colombians and Venezuelans. Several hours later, when I got the text from Sara letting me know all was good, 'he's left kiss kiss,' the guys were still there, either side of me, their eyes still glued to the screen.

# 10: All I want for Christmas

Monday mornings I'd now head into town to visit the girls and collect their commissions. This was my chance to get to know them and the city better. Dividing London at Hyde Park, to the south I'd take in the SWs, Kensington and Knightsbridge, then to the north, the West End and Bond Street.

After weekends spent in my cramped, stuffy man cave, these were days of freedom and movement, exploring-the-city days when I got to pace out the parameters of the business and piece together my mental map of moneyed London, learning how Bayswater connected to Marble Arch, and Knightsbridge slotted into South Ken.

So many of the girls' apartments were close to Hyde Park that on these days its green spaces and wooden benches became my improvised office, and against a backdrop of tourists shuffling through the December chill, I'd be taking bookings and checking which girls were free for a quick catch up. Juggling phones, cigarettes and notepads as I wandered about in aimless circles, those tourists must have wondered what the hell this gibbering lunatic was up to.

When a girl gave me the green light I'd head over to hers, on foot when I had the time, but now recklessly hailing cabs when things were a bit tight. Arriving at their apartments, I'd text them from the street, and while I was waiting for the all clear, I'd be taking in these luxurious neighbourhoods, looking through front windows at the sorts of Christmas trees and festive decorations you'd only expect to find in the West End stores.

Sometimes, on my way in to a girl's apartment, I'd pass a client just leaving, or on my way out I might pass one being buzzed in, oblivious to my role in their little adventure. If the girls had time, I'd stay and chat for a while, taking the chance to catch up on my texts and bookings in a more private and warmer setting, while they updated me on their clients' antics and usually hinted they could handle more work.

Getting everywhere on foot when I had time, I soon learned there was no single millionaire's London, but a crush of wealthy villages, business zones and monuments to conspicuous consumption messily packed up against each other. I'd wander between the girls' apartments marvelling at the mad energy of it all, and the lack of any ordering logic or pattern, unless the pattern was somehow in the chaos.

December was a great time to be heading out into the city. Oxford Street and Regent Street were ablaze now with festive windows and, overhead, the late afternoon skies were glittery with Christmas lights a thousand times brighter than the baubles decking out Wembley High Road. The streets were already rammed with shoppers. Around my old stomping ground of Knightsbridge, I'd smile to myself noticing how many of the couples heading out of the more exclusive stores, and weighed down with their designer bags, were well-dressed older guys with stunning girls who could have been straight from the pages of my website.

Once I'd established my bearings using the major thoroughfares, I'd always try to find alternative, faster routes, and that way I'd stumble across cool record shops and indie book stores hidden away in squeezed-up little side streets, and the best little cafes in London that I'd be in and out of constantly now, grabbing Americanos to ward off the December cold. My favourites were the little wooden huts the cabbies hung out in, dotted all over the city like emerald Tardises.

Every Monday morning I'd set out on this lopsided journey, a CD player anchored in my right jacket pocket, and the earphone on that side dangling loose. That way, I remained alert to the noises of the street, could keep an ear out for my business line and still float through the city on a sonic loop of classic anthems. I had already started to think of Bond themes like You Only Live Twice and Live and Let Die as the soundtrack of my new life.

THE AGENCY

As Amanda, Barry and Rob had all predicted, the run up to the holiday season had already been a bumper one, what with office parties and Christmas bonuses, and a city awash with more money than it knew what to do with, and between now and New Year things were threatening to go atomic. On top of the money flooding into London for the holidays, normal working class sounding guys were calling in who might have been saving up all year for their own little Christmas treat. The phone was pretty much ringing off the hook. I'd already organised a lucrative multiple booking, three girls to The Savoy for an overnighter with a party of Japanese businessmen, so that between going to bed and waking up, and the girls doing their thing, it was officially my best day so far in the business. Funny how quickly this stuff became normal though, and how money you were used to thinking of as a fortune impressed you less when you understood how little it meant to the clients chucking it away.

It was the last Monday before Christmas, and I was reflecting on all this good fortune and hooking up my CD player ready for another foray into the city when Rob called for one of his irregular catch ups, a particularly crackly connection rendering his Essex growl even growlier than usual. Knowing how much he'd appreciate it, I recounted the story of the Savoy booking, listening out through the static for his chuckle of approval.

'Yes, I've had years of that, good luck to yer mate,' he said with obvious relish. 'And how is everything else with you?'

'Really good mate,' I told him, 'I'm getting used to the mix of clients, and the girls' little quirks. They're such a great bunch, to be honest I'm really lucky to have them working with me.'

'So where you gonna be spending all that hard-earned wonga over the holidays?' he asked, and I told him about my plans for the big day; that I'd be at my Auntie Vi's, probably celebrating over a Carry On movie, a turkey for two and a box of luxury crackers. Thanks to my new business venture, Auntie Vi would be doing pretty well out of me this year, I laughingly told him.

'Good lad,' he fired back, 'I'll be thinking of yer when I'm cracking open the Asti Spumante. Yes, I'm out in Barbados mate, bit of a tradition of my own.' I could just picture the scene, Rob all mahogany tan and chunky gold Rolex, entertaining a lovely girl in a private villa overlooking a sparkling ocean, and still not quite able to switch off from the business. 'Are you going to be manning the phones on the big day?' he asked. 'You will get bookings you know, if you want them. Don't forget to check your girls' availability.'

Opening over Christmas hadn't even crossed my mind prior to this call with Rob, and I admitted as much to him. 'Well, my agency's definitely gonna be open, and my girls will be manning the phones', he countered, 'and I can guarantee your girls who are sticking around in London will want the work, even on Christmas Day. And plenty of clients will want to book girls then as well, fuck knows the world rolls on,' he concluded in his engagingly philosophical way.

I was sure he was right, he pretty much always was. I knew maybe two thirds of the girls were staying in London for the holidays, and I guessed they'd be more than happy to cut short their celebrations if a lucrative booking came their way. The others were off enjoying well-earned vacations, mostly with their families, gone from occupying these few square miles of Central London where the streets it seemed really were paved with gold, to the plains and mountain ranges of Brazil, Argentina and Colombia. Almost without exception though, they planned to be back in the New Year for more of the same.

So it was decided then, the Agency would be offering its services even on Christmas day, and I'd be manning the phone over my roast turkey dinner. I just wondered how I was going to explain things to Auntie Vi. I guessed she'd just have to get used to me ducking in and out of the kitchen to discreetly answer the phone at odd moments while I made yet another cup of tea.

'Listen, I just wanted to give you the heads up, let you know you're generating a bit of gossip out there mate,' Rob ran on. 'Word has got round about your new agency, and the charming young British guy running it. Some of the other agency owners have been asking me about you, they tell me your girls say you're lovely, and that you're getting them some great jobs.'

'Oh really? And what have you been telling them?' I quizzed him, with a wry smile. With all I'd learned in the last few months, I instinctively knew Rob would have kept his cards close to his chest. 'I told them never you mind who he is,' he said, in a script I could have written for him, 'he's one of us, he's as good as gold. Anyway, the way it sounds things are going for you, if this was the Oscars, you'd be winning best newcomer. Keep doing what you're doing fella, and I just know 2006 is gonna be a big year for you.'

\*

So close to the holidays now, and with my revised holiday schedule, I was on a bit of a last minute Christmas recruitment drive. Since the site had been up and running, I had only taken on one new girl, Fiona, another gorgeous friend of Amanda's, a Colombian beauty who was based in Covent Garden. Amanda was still proving to be the ultimate resource when it came to getting stunning new girls on board, and she was always pushing me to sign up more, particularly as some, she said, would be heading home for the holidays. She had just let me know a couple of her hometown friends had recently arrived in London. In my imagination this hometown had become a mystical place, exclusively populated by beautiful, dusky maidens with ravenous sexual appetites, and I looked forward to sharing this theory with her when I saw her next. Always the enabler, she'd already found these girls an apartment on the fourth floor of her building, where she had arranged for us to meet and discuss them joining our merry band.

When I arrived, they'd set out coffee and Brazilian pastries, and had been everything Amanda had described them as and more: fun, friendly and flirty. One, Samantha, was a stunning brunette with a Cindy Crawford wholesomeness about her, and the other, Yvonne, a beautiful black girl with a killer body who, as the first 'ebony' escort to join the agency, would prove to be incredibly popular.

Yvonne may only have been in her early twenties, but she was certainly no shrinking violet. Within minutes of my arrival she was giving me a tour of her bedroom, laid out just like Amanda's, with the identical wall of mirrored wardrobes, and had swept open a couple of its doors to show off the results of a self-proclaimed Soho shopping spree. She must have had the full repertoire of outfits in there: sexy nurse, PVC dominatrix, secretary, naughty schoolgirl, policewoman, and in the drawers below this dressing up box of delights a mind-boggling selection of sex toys, all shapes and sizes, all still pristine and in their original boxes. Some, I had no idea what they were even for! This girl clearly wasn't taking any prisoners though, unless of course that was what her clients wanted.

Trying to remain professional, I still couldn't stop my mind from taking odd little fantasy detours, as I imagined her dressed up in these sexy outfits, or pictured her shopping for them in seedy Soho side streets, where emporiums of sexual paraphernalia existed alongside the hipsters sipping their Cappuccinos.

'Tony, I want to ask you,' Yvonne enquired, deferring to my professional judgement and breaking this unprofessional train of thought, 'I want to put mirrors here,' pointing to the ceiling above her bed. 'Is it a good idea?' I told her it sounded like an excellent idea, staring upwards and wondering how the fuck you set about attaching mirrors to a ceiling, and what the handyman she'd have to get in to do the job would make of this little setup.

I'd got everything I needed from the girls in half an hour flat. Stats, preferences, rates and availability had been duly noted in one of my numerous little black notebooks, and their studio shots had been whizzed over to my email account for uploading. This meant that by three o'clock on Monday the nineteenth of December 2005 my agency had officially come of age, now with eighteen ridiculously beautiful and formidably open-minded escorts on its books.

*

I knew that Mondays were Amanda's day to hit the gym, and she'd already texted that morning to say she'd be busy at lunch time 'investing in the body work' as she put it, though how you set about improving on perfection I had no idea. But I had some commission to collect from her and Clarissa, so as I left the new recruits on the fourth floor, I'd sent Clarissa a quick text to see if she was in. She'd responded with a 'yes' and two rows of kisses before I even had time to put my phone back in my pocket, so I headed straight up to hers.

When I reached the apartment, I could see her through its open door, sitting cross-legged on the sofa in her shorts and vest, and leaning avidly into one of her South American soaps, a hand on either side of her face in suspenseful concentration.

Noticing me, she diverted her attention long enough to send a distracted smile and a blown kiss in my direction, and to pick up and fan a stuffed white envelope through the apartment's muggy air. Why, I wondered, were these girl's thermostats always set to a balmy thirty degrees? Were they really trying to turn their Knightsbridge apartment into Copacabana Beach? Remembering Amanda's advice, I counted out the notes and was just stashing them in my breast pocket as the drama reached its awed climax and the titles rolled at breakneck speed. Freed from its hypnotic spell, Clarissa leapt to her feet, overwhelming me with hugs and kisses that still surprised me and left me a little flustered and self-conscious. Amanda was due back any time now, and anyway, she said, still hanging off me, she wanted to tell me about the last client I'd sent her. 'Antonio,' she smiled, 'you would not believe, it was so easy! Four hundred pounds and I massaged his shoulders for the whole hour while he complained his wife didn't understand him. And he didn't even touch me! Once! And then he even gave me a two hundred pound tip on top!' I laughingly commiserated, thinking of all the worse ways there were to earn that kind of money. Were there really guys out there who would pay that for a massage? Was that really what this service was about? Whereas the other girls were less explicit in their comments, none of them seemed to have encountered problems or difficult clients, and the only feedback I was getting from them was how sweet their clients were and how much they'd like to see them again. Where were the problem customers, the difficult bookings that I'd been preparing myself for? Surely sooner or later there would be a problem, though probably better not to think like that.

Just then, Amanda appeared at the door, head to toe in fluorescent gym wear that moulded and cupped every last part of her spectacular body, her hair pulled back in a no nonsense pony tail, and her naked face radiant with the December cold and her post-exercise glow. She gave me a full-on hug and pressed her cheeks softly against mine, her skin warm and cold all at the same time, then dropped her gym bag onto an armchair and headed towards her bedroom. 'I'm so hot and sweaty,' she called back wearily over her shoulder, 'I'm going to jump into the shower.' And then, in a different voice, 'Are you guys going to join me?'

The words hovered in the subdued atmosphere of the apartment, the street noises blowing in from the balcony not enough to dislodge them. *Had she actually said what I thought she had?* I looked across to Clarissa for some sort of corroboration, ready to frame Amanda's question as a stupid joke as soon as she did, if not before, but Clarissa was already excitedly clapping her hands to a chorus of little 'yes, yes, yeses'. By the time I'd turned back to Amanda she was stepping out of her leggings and disappearing into her bedroom, leaving a discarded trail of lycra behind her like a dare. And as I turned back to Clarissa now, my head literally spinning, she too had stripped down to nothing, a tiny fisted ball of vest in one hand and her even tinier crumpled shorts in the other. She skipped excitedly past me and into Amanda's room, only turning at the door's threshold to throw her two little handfuls of fabric in my direction. I, meanwhile, was still fumbling with the belt of my suit trousers, trying to strip and run at the same time, and feeling like the luckiest man in the world while I failed at both.

By the time I'd made it to Amanda's room the girls were already in the shower, two naked goddesses under a misty waterfall, wet and golden against its black marble, and a soft spray already slicking the tangle of their bodies. Clarissa, taller and leaner, her breasts pressed over Amanda's as the girls slid their wet bodies together and the spray settled on their skin and trickled along its curves and recesses.

This was going to be my first threesome, and with two stunning women, one of those things you fantasised about with your mates but knew in your heart of hearts only really belonged in movies. And yet here they were. And here, I had to remind myself, almost pinch myself, I was. Clarissa pushed Amanda's dark hair from in front of her eyes, and they looked out at me as I stood there, taking all of this in, one hand for some reason shielding my dick as it stood to parade ground attention. Realising this was clearly no time for modesty, I let my arm drop to my side and walked towards them in a bit of a daze. As I did so, they stepped apart from each other to wrap themselves around me, skin sliding against skin, their hands circling my chest and shoulders, gently feeling out the descending knots of my back and the ridges of my abs.

Amanda was reaching up to press her soft lips against

mine, biting and pulling, her boobs pressed against me, then her mouth gliding down to graze my shoulder, lick my chest and my waist, and finally sink down on to me. Suddenly Clarissa was there too, their damp, angelic faces smiling up through the fine spray, their hair plastered to their cheeks as one licked the shaft of my dick and the other my balls, and my hands reached down to trace their tanned necks and shoulders, then run over their firm boobs in an ecstasy of choice.

They explored my dick together, over and around, mouths meeting and kissing over its shaft, licking its tip, tongues teasingly sliding across to meet in each other's warm mouths, all the time looking up for signs of tacit pleasure, Clarissa disappearing behind me, her tongue momentarily hot between my legs. Then they were both giggling, and jumping as one out of the shower, and we were all wrapped up against each other in fluffy white bath towels, wet and laughing and giddy with anticipation. Amanda led the way back into the bedroom. She leaned over that epic bed, plumping some pillows against its headboard, then took my hand and sat me back against them, so that I understood this was my front row seat to the show of a lifetime.

Now kneeling across from each other at the foot of the bed, in a perfect symmetry, the girls gradually arched and edged their bodies forward, moving closer until, in a single moment so erotically charged I instinctively moved forwards wanting to be part of it too, their lips were touching. Amanda, aware to every movement, reached a hand out and gently pushed me back to the head of the bed, whispering 'not yet, be patient,' and then in the next moment the girls were pressed hard against each other in a forceful, searching heat that left me breathless.

Amanda was the first to pull away, sliding herself back until she was stretched across the bed, her head tipped provocatively over its side, her arched back accentuating the fullness of her incredible boobs, and now Clarissa was over her, slowly trailing her lips and tongue from mouth to neck to breasts to taut belly, until finally her face was hidden from view between Amanda's legs, and Amanda's soft moans were gradually building, her body betraying the faintest of shudders as her hands gripped at tight knots of fabric in the rumpled sheets. Now Amanda twisted Clarissa onto her back and began the same slow journey down her body, though not content with using her tongue, her fingers followed its trail down between Clarissa's thighs, igniting Portuguese expressions I could only guess at as they fell from her lips in sharp little exhalations.

It would be easy to write it was like being part of the most incredible porn film, but it was so much more than that. I'd never seen girls as hot, or as passionate as this, in any of the videos I'd ever watched. When Amanda finally raised her head, Clarissa twisted around onto her hands and knees,

Amanda caressing her body, licking her boobs, biting her full lips. Finally, she took my hand and prompted me to my part, guiding it over her friend's body, leading it wherever she wanted without the least resistance from Clarissa, just the occasional involuntary quiver, as we travelled over her firm breasts and responsive nipples, as our hands glided over her taut belly and slid between her legs searching out the wet heat, then after a moment's hesitation pressed lower between her smooth, spread cheeks, gently massaging and gaining a tight traction.

It was Amanda who reached for the bottle of lube and gently massaged Clarissa's tight hole while, in disbelief, I ripped open one of those little silver packets. Then it was Amanda again who acted as guide, spreading Clarissa before me, gripping me hard and pressing me into her as she tensed, then shuddered and finally relaxed, and it was Amanda's lips pressed against mine as I lost myself in the moment, watching the fantasy playing out on the mirrored wardrobes across from us, wondering whether watching made it more or less real, more or less dreamlike.

I watched our three tangled bodies rising and falling as one, took in the reflected rhythmical thrusts, the girls' curves and ellipses and my leaner, more angular shape. I watched Amanda laying her lips on mine, showering me with little bites of kisses as I heard Clarissa in her delirium intoning 'harder,

harder'. I watched as finally Clarissa pulled away and rolled onto her back, and as Amanda slipped off the condom, and coaxingly pushed me towards her friend's mouth. I watched as Amanda joined her there beneath me, as their lips parted in anticipation and I came over their faces.

\*

The girls had disappeared into the bathroom and I was stretched out on Amanda's bed staring at the ceiling and wondering if I was about to wake up from this incredible dream, when Amanda sauntered back into the bedroom naked, lit a cigarette and placed it between my lips, Clarissa, hot on her heels, lay back down beside me smiling her mischievous Brazilian smile, and in the slow, sensual comedown I started to take in the reality of what had just happened, and everything that was about to happen.

These were the dying days of 2005, and I was lying between two naked Goddesses in a luxury South Ken apartment. In the sudden quiet of Amanda's bedroom I listened to the sounds of slow, sweaty breathing mixing with the noises of the city rising from the street, just as they used to rise to the Harrods roof terrace.

The sounds set me thinking back over the last six months, all the events playing through my mind in a sequence of flashbacks: the weeks of lusting over Amanda on that sultry summer rooftop, our first conversation, the party in this apartment that had changed everything. Then meeting Barry and Rob, and the improbable events that had somehow led to me finding myself right here right now.

I was thinking about the things I'd done and seen, thought and felt, and about the equally improbable New Year that was waiting for me on the other side of this holiday. Thinking about how it was holding all its secrets to itself, both the good and the bad. With no idea quite how much of both lay ahead.

Made in the USA
San Bernardino, CA
14 January 2018